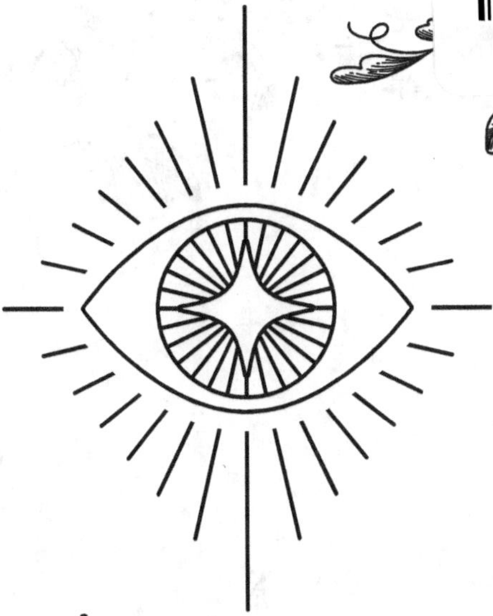

A Girl with the Third Eye!

By

Palak Kashyap

This book is a work of fiction. Names,
characters, businesses, organizations,
places, events,
and incidents either are the product of the
author's imagination or are used
fictitiously.
Any resemblance to actual persons, living
or dead, events, or locales is entirely

coincidental.

Copyright © 2023 by Palak Kashyap

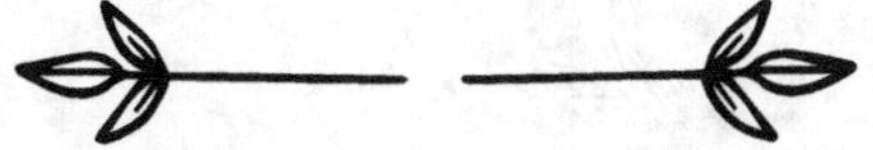

"To my dearest mum, who always believed in me and encouraged me to follow my dreams. Though you are no longer with me in this world, your love and support continue to inspire me every day. Without your guidance, I would not be where I am today. You were not just my mother, but also my mentor, my confidence and my best friend. Your unwavering faith in me gave me the courage to pursue my passion for writing, and I know that you would be proud of the book that I have written.

I wish you were here to see the final product, to see how all your love and support have culminated in this work, But I know that you are still with me in spirit guiding me and watching over me.

I dedicate this book to you, Mum, as a small tribute to all that you have done for me. Thank you for everything and may your soul rest in peace."

"A Girl with the third eye" is a captivating and mystical tale that follows the extraordinary journey of Peace, a young girl who discovers she possesses a unique and powerful gift- a third eye. Set in a world where strong intuitions and reality intertwined, Peace's third eye allows her to see beyond the physical realm and delve into the depths of the spiritual and supernatural.

As Peace navigates her way through the complexities of adolescence, she grapples with the challenges of understanding and harnessing her extraordinary abilities. Peace learns to control her third eye and tops into its immense potential.

Throughout the book, Peace encounters dark forces and unveils the truth about her own origins. Along the way, she forms deep friendships, faces personal trials and discovers the importance of trust, bravery and self acceptance.

"A Girl with the Third Eye" is a thrilling, horror and enchanting tale that explores themes of self-discovery, destiny and the power of embracing one's uniqueness. Filled with vivid imagery, compelling characters and unexpected twists, this book will captivate readers of all ages.

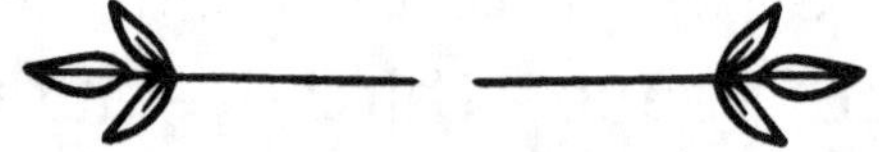

A Girl with the Third Eye!

Have you ever encountered something unnatural? Something which is dark and evil, And what if I tell you that I "Peace" can see them, I don't know if it's a gift to me or a curse but I can see them.....

I don't know when and how it started but it's something that makes me wonder why God has chosen me? I am living in continuous fear of what I am going to encounter next...
This is my journey which was designed by my destiny. I am the chosen one who is blessed with the power of a third eye where I can feel and see the entities who are seeking help and by helping them I discovered myself.

I still remember I was 7 years old when I first encountered something which totally changed my life. Imagine being a kid who encountered something evil and dark and you can't even express what you just dealt with because no one is going to believe you.....

I was a very mischievous kid back then and an only kid to my parents, I was so over pampered by my mom and dad. I had my own little world full of colors like every little girl has in their childhood. Dad just bought a new house and we shifted here two months back and Mom and I both were excited to decorate our new nest. We were so happy with the location, Mom grabbed my hand and showed me the beautiful part of our new home which she just decorated herself. It was the garden which she decorated herself with every plant you can think of.

She had decorated the place with Roses, Tulips, Daisies, Sunflowers and what not and in one corner I saw a small playhouse which is designed as a Castle. I was very overwhelmed with what I saw and I hugged my mom so tightly, She creased my messy hair from my face and asked me if I liked it or not?
I asked her "Dad made this for me?"
Which she replied "Yes! Princess"...

I ran up to the playhouse and walked up the stairs and opened the door. Mom decorated my play house so beautifully, there was a small princess throne chair, toys, books and my stuffed toys. It was my small world and I loved it and seeing me enjoying every bit of that place Mom was happy too. It was evening by now and Dad also came back from the office and he picked me up in his arms and asked me if I liked my surprise or not? I gave Dad a peck on his cheeks and told him that I loved it....

For me, my new playhouse is the place where I spend most of the time playing there, but I have no clue what's coming next!

I Came back from the School, after taking a good nap I came down to my living room, Mom was in the kitchen. She asked me, if I wanted to eat something?
To which I replied " No! Mum, I am good."
Mom was busy preparing dinner and I turned on the television...

I was enjoying my cartoons. Suddenly I heard something from the backyard where our garden was to which I ran to my mom and told her that I heard a loud thump noise from the backyard!
To which she responded it must be a cat or something else. Just ignore it. Dad is about to come and will see later what it was and she locked the backyard door and told me to go upstairs and finish my homework to which I responded "Ok!"

Dad came back home from the office later that night and we were all at the dinner table. I told Dad about the incident to which he also responded the same as Mom. Being a stubborn kid I keep on asking Dad to check the backyard because I was worried about my playhouse....
After finishing the dinner, Dad went out to check the backyard and me & mom followed him. I was praying in my mind for my Castle to be safe and sound.

Dad turned on the lights of the backyard. To our surprise we saw that someone just broke the flower pots which were kept near to my playhouse's door. Both the pots were broken as if someone lifted and threw them off from there to ground and my playhouse was on height, let me tell you there were stairs to climb for the entrance of the playhouse's door and it was impossible for a cat to drop those heavy pots from there that too, two pots in one go and which is kept in distance from each other, it was so unusual because i remember i heard only one loud noise...
Dad checked my Playhouse and everything was kept as it is.

I was so relaxed that my Castle was ok, but who dropped the pots? Dad and Mom both were convinced that it might be a wild cat or a raccoon that might have dropped those pots and we went inside and being a kid I also forgot about the incident as my Castle was safe so I was relaxed. We went inside and called off the day.

Two days passed by and nothing happened, but on the evening of the third day I saw something which made me hate my playhouse the most.....
I came down to the living room looking for Mom, but she was not there i tried looking for her everywhere in the house but she was nowhere to be seen, i thought she must have been gone out for the groceries or so, but she never left me alone in the house before without even telling me, I thought there must be something really important. I turned on the television and started watching my cartoons. It must have been 15 or 20 minutes passed by. I heard a loud bang noise again from the backyard and I was so scared to the moment as I was alone in the entire house, I ran towards the backyard door and locked it.

 Then i thought it must be Mom working in the backyard so i took a stool and climbed on it and peeked through the window and to my surprise i saw mom standing in front of my playhouse's door and her face was towards the door all i could see her from the back, i came down from the stool and opened the back door and ran towards my mom and was continuously calling her but she was not responding me so, i went to her and i hugged her from behind and started crying because i was so scared and started complaining her that i was looking for her in the entire house and how could you do this with me, but to my surprise she was not responding me. She was standing still there facing towards the door.

I kept calling her but she was not even listening to me so I shook her hand. I noticed something really different, her hand was looking so pale and it was cold. I kept on shaking her hand and that was the moment when she turned back! It was not Mom! It was a spine chilling moment for me. The Lady turned back and gave me a strong push and I rolled down the stairs and I don't know what happened next it was all blackout for me......

When I woke up I saw dad and mum were sitting next to me and my head was spinning and paining very badly.

I asked Mom " Mommy why are you crying?"
To which she hugged me tightly and kissed my forehead gently.
She Replied "Nothing princess!"
Dad Asked me, " Princess, how did this happen?"
To which I replied " Happened! What Dadda?"

Dad was a bit confused and I could see concern in his eyes. Mum had tears in her eyes and she was looking at me with concern.
I asked Dad "Dadda why is my head paining badly?"
To which he replied "Princess what happened to you at the playhouse and how you fell off from the stairs of it?"
I recalled everything and I asked Dad "Dad where is she gone?"
Dad replied "Who?"

There was an utter silence in the room. Everyone was confused.
I told dad "Dadda! There was a lady, she was standing near my castle's door. I was looking for mum and i thought mum was standing there but when i approached her she was not answering me, her hands were pale and cold and suddenly she turned back and pushed me and all i remember that i rolled down from the stairs and after that i couldn't remember anything."
Mom and Dad were shocked!

Who was that lady and why did she push me from the stairs?
This was the first encounter and my world was by now upside down.......
They thought I was daydreaming or must be making stories but I had no words to express what I actually saw!

Few days passed by and I still remember I was sitting on the bench in the garden and Mom was watering the grass and I saw that lady again peeking through my castle window. I was stunned the very first time I could actually see her face and to my shock it was the face I can't forget for the rest of my life......

I saw her face was covered with blood and it was looking as if her skin was rotten and she had no eyes, it was all black hollow space in the place of her eyes and she was peeking through the window. For a couple of minutes I froze there. I wanted to call Mom but I don't know why words were not coming out of my mouth and my eyes were glued on the window of my castle. Out of fear I started crying and yelling, to which my mom heard me and she came running towards me and picked me up in her arms and asked me what was wrong with me?

I told her what I saw and she thought i'm just creating stories. She went there to check the castle but to my surprise no one was there. I was so terrified and i just wanted to go inside the house, i insisted mom to take me inside and she did the same, she gave me water and want me to settle down in my bed and i did the same without uttering any words, i grabbed her finger and took her with me to my room and told her to stay with me as i was so scared with what i just saw.

Mom agreed and we came into my room, she was moving her fingers in my hair to calm me down and i don't know when i slept, Suddenly in my dreams i saw that rotten face again and i started crying in my sleep, i was shouting and crying so badly that my mother woke me and hugged me tight and i was still crying, I told her i saw that lady again in my dreams, to which she hugged me even more tight and made sure that everything is alright its just a dream.

Mom noticed that am having a high fever and she panicked and called Dad and in no time Dad was there. Dad took the half day from the office that day, and they both were so worried that why am I behaving like this, Mom was placing cold strips of cloth on my forehead so that my temperature would go down. They called a doctor too and he said it might be a seasonal flu and gave me the medicines. I know I was not imagining anything but why does mom and dad not believe me?

The kid who used to be more cheerful and playful now becomes a kid who used to sit in the corner. I chose not to speak to anyone because the whole incident traumatized me and I was shattered from inside, no one was believing me and moreover what I saw was not easy to digest. Mom and Dad were now concerned about me and Mom made sure every time that i'm ok or not and she was giving me extra care and love. In a few days I was out of that trauma but now I was scared of the place which was my small world, where I used to spend my time playing there with my toys, now I can't even have the guts to even look at it.

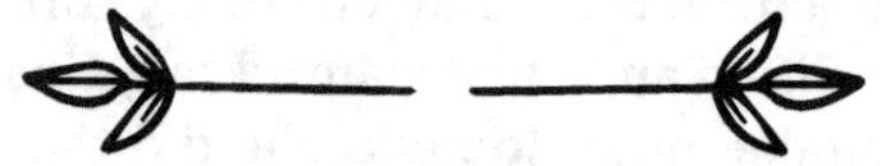

I was so traumatized by the whole event. Being a kid and witnessing something out of the world experience which has no evidential aspects, I am keen to solve the mystery of this whole unsolved scenario of this Lady!
"Who was She?"
 "What does she want from me?"
"Why can only I see her?"

It's been a month and it seems everything is settled as if for now, Mom and dad were giving extra time to me. I was enjoying my time with them and I totally forgot about the incident which happened a month back. Mom and dad decided to dismantle the playhouse as they thought it might help me to get out of the trauma. I agreed upon their decision as I started disliking the playhouse and never went back after that event so in a way I was satisfied with my parents decision.

.A few weeks went by and everything was going well, it was my Dad's birthday and me and mum decided to give him a birthday surprise party. So, we decided that we will decorate our garden. In the middle of the garden there was a sitting porch where the sittings were so we decided that we will keep the birthday cake there and when dad comes home after work we will take him to the backyard garden and give him a surprise. Everything was going as we planned, we decorated the entire place with balloons and mom baked the cake and I helped her with the cake decorations. I was super excited and was waiting for my dad so eagerly. I wore my favorite white and pink floral dress and dressed up for the party.

My eyes were on the clock and now it was the time when dad

was about to come from the office. We did last minute preparations. Doorbell rang and I saw that dad was back, I ran towards him and hugged him with all my love and he picked me up and I pecked on her cheeks and wished him.
"Happy Birthday Dadda!"

Dad kissed my forehead and replied "Thank you my love."
I told dad to get me down and he did and I grabbed his arms and took him to the backyard and me and mom shouted loudly -"Surprise!"
"Happy Birthday Dadda!"
Dad kissed my forehead and replied "Thank you my love."
I told dad to get me down and he did and I grabbed his arms and took him to the backyard and me and mom shouted loudly -"Surprise!"

It was the middle of the night i woke up to strange cracking noise which was coming from my room only and i was so scared the i shut my eyes tightly and grabbed my quilt with my both hands, but i would still hear the noise i tried peeking through the quilt that were the sound is coming from, the room was partly dark and i could see in the light of my side lamp that someone was present in my room and i mustered my courage and tried to inspect that from where the noise is coming and it was from the rocking chair which was kept near my bed on the left side of the window.

I could see someone was sitting on the chair and to my surprise it was mum. But in the back of my mind it strikes that why mum is here and what is she doing in my room in the middle of the night ?? It was unusual. I got up from my bed and asked mom-
"Hey mom! Is everything alright ?"
To which mum kept quiet. I again asked her
"Mom is that you?"
"Hello!"
Still no answer from mum, i asked again-
"Mom, what are you doing here? Please answer me.."
"Mom, I'm scared now, Please stop it. It's not funny."

wThe rocking chair stopped moving and I could see mom was now sitting still in the chair. I was so scared and froze there for a second. It felt like I skipped my heartbeat and all I could feel was that my heart would come out of my mouth as it was beating so fast.

I was in great terror and the whole room was in dead silence and all I could hear was my heartbeat. I again grabbed my courage and asked again-

"Mom, is that you?"

To which i heard a whisper from here mouth

"Are you Scared?"

To which I was shocked and there was silence all around. I wanted to talk but it was like no words were coming out of my mouth and I was standing still there as if I was frozen.

She stood from her place and turned towards me, I could see in the low light, her hair was flowing all over her face and she started walking slowly towards me. As she was walking towards me I started seeing her in the dim light of my lamp. Her skin was so pale but due to darkness I couldn't see her face. As she approached me I could see a different face, It was not my mother!

Her face was pale and she had long black hair which was flowing all over her face. I was so shocked and scared that I don't know when and how my tears started rolling over my cheeks but i don't have the courage to say anything or to react, I was standing there like a dummy.

She was standing in front of me. I wanted to cry and run from there but I couldn't move a single step in terror. She whispered again-

"Get out!"

And she repeatedly said the same thing and her voice started increasing and it was the time when I couldn't bear the intensity of her voice and it started hurting my ears. I put both my hands over my ears and I shouted at the top of my lungs- "Please stop it " and started crying loudly, my whole body was shivering. And everything vanished as if there was no one in the room. By the time mom and dad heard me crying they came running towards my room and dad turned on the light and mom comforted me and asked me what am i doing and why am I out of my bed in the middle of the night? I was shivering like anything and I was feeling so scared that I was not able to stop myself from crying. Dad hugged me and asked me if I was alright? Once I caught my breath I told mom and dad "I saw her!"

Mom replied- "Who?"
I told her " The Lady!"
Dad said "Baby, there is no one. You saw who?"
I said in my stumbling voice "The Playhouse Lady"
Mom and dad e both were having looked at each other and there was a moment of silence in the whole room.

Dad breaks the ice and says
 "Princess! Calm down. We are with you, please relax."
I gave them the acceptance by nodding my head. I could sense the concern on my parents' faces, however that night nobody slept and I got a high fever which lasted about a week and I was feeling so weak as if someone was sucking out all my energy.

By this time I was so afraid of being alone cause I don't want to see that lady again. On one such day, I was sitting in my living room, mom was cooking dinner in the kitchen and dad was in his study room (must be working on his official deadlines). I was enjoying my cartoon shows and suddenly I heard that someone knocked on our back door. I told mom that someone is at our door, to which she came out from the kitchen and she also witnessed that there is someone out there knocking our back door, but how is it possible there is no other way that one could access the backyard without coming in from our main door. She ran towards the door and locked it and told me to call my dad from his study room and by the time she will lock every door and window.

The knocking sound was coming continuously from the back door and me and mom both panicked and now with every minute the knocking sound is getting louder and louder. I ran towards my dad's study room and told everything that was happening downstairs with us, to which dad immediately ran towards the living room to help mom. He also witnessed the continuous banging knocks coming from the back.

Everyone was scared and dad decided that he would go and check who it could possibly be. Mom was not okay with dad's idea and she told dad that it will be a bad idea if he will do so , he can't risk everyone's life like that and suggested that we should call the emergency helpline. To which dad was agreed on. By this time the knocking noise went louder. Dad decided to peek from the window and see who possibly it could be because someone was knocking the door so aggressively. Dad went to the window and to his surprise nobody was there but the knocking was still there on the door. Mom called the emergency help line and asked for help. Dad was shocked and froze there.

 I could see that there was something wrong because I could see fear in his eyes. Mom rushed towards him and told him that help was on the way but dad was not saying anything as if he was in a state of shock. And suddenly the knocking was over, there was silence in the room as everybody was waiting for the officers to come. We sat on the couches while waiting for the officers and I screamed loudly because I saw her again in the window. She was smirking at me from the window, it was the time i lost it and i started yelling like anything at the window.

I yelled at the top of my lungs and told that mysterious lady to leave us alone but she was still there and looked at me with a devilish smile. Mom and dad asked me what am I looking at and why am I yelling to which I told them that there is that playhouse lady at our backyard window and she is standing there and looking at us. Mom and dad were confused as they couldn't see anybody there. I told them
"Look! She is there and she is smiling."
And suddenly there was a loud bang on the window. Everyone was stunned, i told mom and dad.

"She is angry and she wants us to get out of this house else she

will kill us."
With that there was a loud bang again at the window and this time it was so impactful that the window's glass was cracked. Dad grabbed me and we three ran towards the kitchen. The bell rang and we saw that the officers arrived. Dad ordered mom to stay with me here in the kitchen and he went out to see the officers.

There were 2 officers who came to help us, Dad told them everything and they came inside and investigated the whole backyard but there was no one. They also saw the broken window and suggested to us that there were no forced entry and nobody could access the place and they were also shocked. One of the officers came to me and asked me what I saw to which I told him everything and told him that I saw this lady often and she wanted us out of this place. officers noted down the details and told us that till the time they investigate we should stay at safe place and advised us to go to our family, friends or possible can stay at hotel till the time everything is sorted to which dad agreed and we immediately took our necessary belongings and packed our bags and we took a hotel room.

Mom and Dad were comforting me and we were so traumatized with the whole thing which we faced. Anyhow, we slept that night in the hotel, but trust me I got a great sleep after so many days. There was no one I should be scared of and I was so relaxed that we are not in that house anymore.

In the afternoon, dad received a call from the officer and he asked if we could meet him, to which dad agreed and we left to the place where he called us. It was a coffee shop where the officer wanted us to meet. So, we took a spot there and a few minutes later the officer also arrived. we could see that the officer was also looking a bit concerned, to which dad asked him if everything was ok! Did he have any clue ?
To which officer Ellen replied-
"I want you to see a photograph and show the same photograph to Peace also. Before I tell you the further details, Peace should identify if she has seen any of these people there in the house."

Officer showed me an old picture. I still remember it was an old picture of a family, there was a little boy with his mother and father. I immediately recognised the lady in the picture as it was the lady which I was seeing in my house. I told the officer Ellen while pointing at that lady's face that she is the one I am seeing in my house. Mom and Dad were still looking confused and both were waiting for the officer Ellen to conclude the whole thing. On the other hand I could see officer Ellen's forehead creased and he was looking shocked as if he had never been in the same position before. There was an awkward silence between us. While mom and dad were waiting for the answers from Officer Ellen.

Officer Ellen took a deep breath and then told us about the lady's story. Her name was Trisha Woods, Her husband Mr... Denial Woods was a businessman and together they had a child named Ron woods. They were the happiest family one could dream of, Trisha was a housewife and Ron was around Seven years old. Trisha loves to take care of her family, they mean the whole world to her. Mr... Denial was a well known businessman.

.Six years ago, we got an emergency call from Mr... Woods' neighbors that they heard Mr.. and Mrs.. Woods were having an argument and Mrs. Wood was screaming at that time so they called the Emergency helpline so that we could settle the matter.

Officer Ellen added that back then he and Officer Raven went to Mr.. Woods house and on arriving they questioned Mr.. Woods about the same, that the neighbors had complained against them regarding the domestic violence, to which Mr... Denial denied the charges against him. Officer Raven questioned Mrs. Woods too, in which she also said that everything was fine. It was just a misunderstanding that they two had and they were having an argument other than that they were fine. To which we gave them warning and left.

Then Dad furiously asked " Officer Ellen!
Can you please come to the point, How this is relatable with what we are facing in our house?"
Officer Ellen replied "It is relatable!"
Mom asked "How?"

Officer Ellen again took a deep breath and looked right into my dad's eyes and replied- " Your house" and he took a pause to which my Dad asked- " Our house????"
Mom and Dad both were looking confused and I could see that Officer Ellen was looking uncomfortable while narrating everything.

Mom asked Mr.. Ellen " Please Officer! Tell us the truth, how is this correlated to our house?"
Officer Ellen replied- "The house where you are living in was once owned by Mr.. Woods."
Mom and Dad looked at each other and then they both looked and Officer Ellen to which he said- " I know you guys are having lots of questions in your mind right now i will answer your every questions but for now i have to take a leave because i have to go and i will meet you guys in your home tomorrow with Officer Raven and we will be accountable to every questions of yours but i suggest you should stay in the hotel for tonight also." To which Dad nodded his head and then Officer Ellen left us in hurry. We came back to our hotel room and I could see mom and dad were trying to hide fear on their faces and now I could tell what they might be going through.

Next day in the morning Dad received a call from Officer Ellen and he told us to meet outside our house at 3 PM. We did what Mr.. Ellen said and we met Officer Ellen and Officer Raven outside our house. We went inside our home and gathered in our living room. There was an awkward silence, Dad broke the ice and questioned Mr.. Ellen - "Officer Ellen now can you please tell us what is wrong with this place?"

To which Officer Ellen was about to answer but Officer Raven cut him in between and told my Dad that She would tell us everything but before that she wanted my mom to take me inside, to which mom ordered me to go upstairs to my room. I acted like i went upstairs but i was so curious to know everything so i sat in the corner of the stairs where mom and dad can't see me. I can hear them speaking, Officer Raven started telling dad about our house's history.

She Told Mom and Dad that when they warned Mr.. and Mrs. Woods about the whole thing they left their house but soon after two months Mr.. Woods filed a missing complaint against his wife and son. On investigating he handed us a letter written by Mrs. Wood that she doesn't want to be with him and she is leaving Mr.. Woods house and taking their kid with her. Officer Ellen added that they investigated their family and friends but nobody was agreeing on the fact that Mrs. Wood could do this as she loved her family so much and she was an amazing house wife.

Her mother stated that " How could Tarisha can leave the house she made herself, she made that entire place a home with her hands from every little details she gave her personal touch to the house, she made the house a home, she cant leave everything like that and if she left she had no other one to stay with she is so closed to me she have had came or told me before taking this step."

Officer Raven said - "In fact, everyone in their family and friends were agreed with Tarisha's mother's statement."

Mom asked - "Then what happened? Did you find her?"

Officer Ellen replied - "No! It's still a mystery where they went and what happened to her and her son."

Officer Raven added - " It was strange that after one year we received a call from Mr.. Woods' neighbors that they heard a gunshot from Mr.. Woods backyard house and upon arrival we investigated and found Mr.. Woods' dead body.
He shot himself and further upon investigation we found that Mr.. Wood lost his mental state after his wife left him."

Officer Ellen added- " Mr.. Woods's neighbors stated that they have seen him talking to himself and they heard him screaming in the middle of the night. We investigate but due to lack of Evidence we declared it Suicide and closed the case."

Officer Raven said - " Officer Ellen said that your daughter identified Mrs. Woods in the photograph as she saw her in your house! How's that possible?"
They were discussing the whole thing and in between i suddenly felt a cold breeze on my left shoulder as if someone passed from my side. I quickly ran into my room out of fear and closed the door and jumped on my bed and hid myself under the blanket. I heard footsteps near my bed, I was shaking in terror and I don't know when but out of fear I started crying and hoping everything would end so that I could run downstairs.

I wanted to scream and call Mom and Dad but out of fear words were not coming out of my mouth. Then the footsteps stopped near me and then everything felt silent. I wanted to peek out from my blanket but I decided not to because I was so scared. I heard a woman's voice, whispering something near my ear. By this time I was so scared that I was about to faint but I don't know what kept me awake. I heard her repeating the same line - "He Lied, He broke my Trust! I killed him."

I don't know where I got the strength and I questioned her - "Is that you Mrs. Woods?"
There was no answer. I asked her again in a stumbling voice "Is that you Mrs. Woods? I heard them talking about you. What do you want from me?"

Still there was no answer, so i thought she left so i took a deep breath and planned in my mind how i am gonna jump from my bed and run downstairs to mom and dad. The moment I took my blanket off I saw her sitting in front of me on the chair which was kept a few steps away from me.
This was the time I felt like I'm gonna die for a second but when I saw her I saw sadness in her eyes and instead of getting scared I felt instantly connected to her. Being a kid I asked her in an innocent way "Are you fine Mrs. Woods? Why are you sad?" I can see pain in her eyes and at that moment I felt so connected that I forgot that I was scared just a few minutes before.

I saw a different side of Mr.. Woods spirit . Now she was not angry, in a loving way she replied- "Please help me love!"
To which I replied - "How?"
She replied - " I want Peace."
I replied - " How can you have me? Do you want to eat me?"
To which she gave a smile and replied " Please tell your Mom and Dad to look for a Red Diary which has a gold rose embossed on its front cover. It's in the study chamber."
With this she smiled and vanished into thin air.

I ran downstairs and saw mom and dad were still talking with the Officers seeing me running like this they asked me "Is everything alright with me?" To which i told them everything which just happened with me in my room. Mom hugged me tightly and started crying. I asked mom what was wrong with her to which she hugged me again. Dad then said that we should look for that Red Diary in the study chamber and everybody ran towards the study chamber in search of that Diary which was holding our every question.

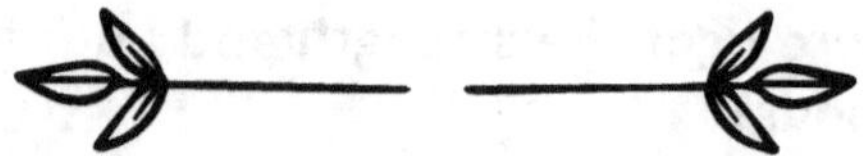

4

We started searching for the diary, everyone was looking at every book closely so that they could find the diary but it's nowhere to be seen. every book, every shelf and even drawers we searched.

And at last we got tired and Dad said it's just a waste of time and I must be cooking stories because if there will be a diary here they could have got it as they have searched every single corner of that place. First time i saw my dad's anger, he had frustration in his eyes, i know we were going through tough time and it is evident that anybody can get frustrated in such situations, now i can understand my dad's situation at that time being and adult now but at that time i was a kid and seeing dad like that I couldn't control my emotions and i started crying to wish dad apologized me and hugged me he said he is mentally and physically drained because of this situation. Officer Ellen asked me if there was anything special which Mrs. Woods told me, To which I recalled everything and told him that "Yes! she told me the diary had a golden rose embossed on it."

Dad said "We searched every book here but there is not a single one which had this golden Rose on it."
Suddenly my eyes caught something and I shouted loudly, "Dad look on the Wall There is a Golden Rose."

There was a canvas painting of a Golden rose in the wall and dad took that painting off from the wall and to our surprise there was a small diary stuck behind the canvas. It was a beautiful Diary which had a red velvety outer cover and a golden rose was embossed on the middle of the front cover. Officer Raven took that Diary from my Dad and inspected it and then we all gathered in the living room again. Officer Raven told us that this was Mrs. Woods personal Diary.

Dad asked officer Raven - " Can we read this?"

To which the Officer nodded her head and opened the Diary, It was the Diary which Mrs. Woods used to write, She has mentioned everything in that diary. Officer Raven started reading it out loud and everyone was glued there because they wanted to know the truth about Trisha's past.

Mrs.. Woods wrote " My life was a blank canvas before, I was an introvert and I have seen my mother being a Housewife, she and dad shared a strong relationship and I always admired my man to be like my dad, He knows how to balance his professional and private life. Mom and dad were the perfect couple and both love each other so much that seeing them like this from childhood had made me picture my partner to be perfect like my Dad. Then I met Daniel at my mom and Dad's anniversary celebration. He was my Dad's project partner's son.

Dad introduced me to Mr... Willam and his son Danial and that is how we met and instantly fell in love with each other. I saw my dad in him, A perfect gentleman! We got married and I could say that this is the life I dreamt of. He was the nicest person to me and slowly and gradually became my world.

We saw many ups and down but Daniel never let me down in any aspects of our married life. We enjoyed each other's company and then after 2 years we welcomed our son into this world and we named him "Ron". On Ron's birth Daniel gifted me this House. It was our love nest and to me it was the most beautiful gift I could ever imagine. From the decors to the plants I placed everything from my hands and this was our nest. I fell in love with everything here and to me now this is my small world. Daniel, Me and Ron and our happy place. We have had the best life but suddenly my whole world went upside down. How can Daniel do this with me, after 9 years of our marriage and all the happy moments we have had with each other.

We saw many ups and down but Daniel never let me down in any aspects of our married life. We enjoyed each other's company and then after 2 years we welcomed our son into this world and we named him "Ron". On Ron's birth Daniel gifted me this House. It was our love nest and to me it was the most beautiful gift I could ever imagine. From the decors to the plants I placed everything from my hands and this was our nest. I fell in love with everything here and to me now this is my small world. Daniel, Me and Ron and our happy place. We have had the best life but suddenly my whole world went upside down. How can Daniel do this with me, after 9 years of our marriage and all the happy moments we have had with each other.

I always saw Daniel as the perfect gentleman, the man I always dreamt of as a partner just shattered me to the core. It all started when Daniel was giving extra time to his work. He changed himself, the person who always looks after us has started giving the cold shoulder to us. Every day we waited for him to be back home for dinner but not everything changed. He started giving us befitting replies to everything which I asked him. Then the day came when everything went meaningless for me, my entire relationship with him went meaningless.

I saw Daniel and his Secretary in an awkward position in our own home, in our own study chamber and it felt like my world stopped there. Rest at night we had a bad argument and for the very first time he raised his hand over me. I am done with this relationship, I am done with this man and I want to overcome this and I will take Ron and leave him alone because he doesn't deserve us! Daniel doesn't deserve us! He broke my trust, I will never forgive him."

And the rest of the pages in the diary were empty. There was an envelope kept in the last page of the diary. Officer Raven took that envelope out and on the front side of the envelope it was written "I Am Sorry Love!"

Dad took that envelope from Officer Raven and asked if he could read it loud. To which officer Raven agreed. Dad opened the envelope and it was a letter written by Mr.. Woods in which he confessed something which solved everything which was kept in the dark for six years.

Mr.. Woods wrote- " I am sorry Tarisha and Ron for doing this to you. I know there are no apologies which can coverup my sins. Yes I did a Sin and now it's haunting me every day, every night and every second of my life. Your words are haunting me and I can't take this anymore. I rewarded your loyalty and love with my disloyalty. I know I did wrong but it's too late to undo what I did. I wish I could go in the past and change it but it's too late for me to get you back. I am sorry, I hope we meet on the other side soon."

The moment dad finished reading the letter I don't know what happened to me but all of the sudden my head felt a sharp pain and i started feeling dizzy. Mom grabbed me in her arms and she was asking me something but at that moment my ears were blocked, my vision was blurred and I saw a flashback of something which solved every question for us.

I saw a flashback of Mrs. Wood's life. I saw how she had a banter with Mr.. Woods over Abby. Abby was the secretary of Mr.. Woods. I had a vision that Mrs. Woods saw them in the office and she slapped Me.. woods and ran from there. The next scene I saw that Mr.. and Mrs. Woods were having an argument and It seems that Mrs. Woods had a panic attack and they were both yelling at each other. I saw Officer Raven and Officer Ellen on the Door.

The nxt scene I saw was about Mrs. Woods and Ron, where Mrs. Woods had her suitcase in her hand and with the other hand she was holding her Son's hand. It seems that Mrs. Woods is going somewhere with her child and Mr.. Wood was stopping them. Mrs. Woods was about to leave the room and was going down stairs but in the tif with Mr.. Woods, she and Ron tumbled from the stairs and due to heavy suitcase Ron got a injury in his head and the blood was dripping from his head and Mrs. woods is also got injury and she is sitting near the body of his son and crying as if that the boy passed away on the spot because of the injury.

The next scene I saw that again Mr.. and Mrs. Woods had an aggressive argument and to which Mrs. Woods went near the Telephone, she was about to grab the receiver and Mr.. Woods hit her with the vase on her backside of her head and while crying he dragged both the bodies to his backyard. Mrs. Wood was still alive when he buried her and his son in the backyard and soon after he built a backyard house over it so that no one could ever know what he was hiding there. He reported the missing report of his wife and son but the guilt made him take his own life there where he buried the bodies of his family.

With a sudden shake I got into my senses and narrated everything which I saw, the place where Mr.. Woods buried the body of Mrs. Woods and Ron was the place where my play house was. Everyone was shocked and Officer Ellen said they should call the team and discuss this matter and next day we saw Officer Ellen and Officer Raven was there with the team, they came up with the legal warrant to dig that place and upon further investigating that place they found two bodies.

When I thought everything was over, I saw Mrs. Woods again but this time I was not scared of her. She saw me and with a smile she vanished in a white light. Finally she rested in peace.

This was the start of my life's journey, the journey with the third eye. The third eye which can see what others can't.

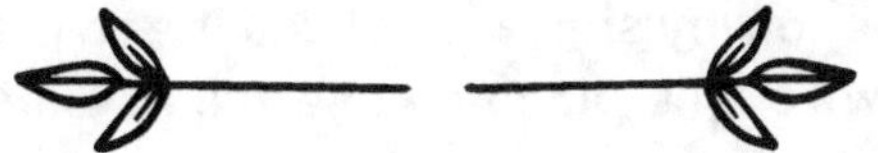

5

After this whole incident, a few months later dad decided to shift the house because we have gone through so much in the past few months. So dad bought a lake house for us so that we could start our lives again and forget all that happen to us in the past. we reached the place and everything was so calm there, the lake, the house and everything was giving us all the pleasant vibes. The caretaker of the house named "Miller" was also nice to us and he was a super friendly guy, he must be in his mid twenties. He takes care of that place and he was the local of that place, so he knows everything about the place and people. It was a small town so people were very generous and friendly and the whole town had an amazing peaceful vibe. Greens everywhere, clear sky, fresh air it seems heavenly there.

Our lake house was also very beautiful, Miller was taking care of the house and Anna was the house helper. She was also from that town. I met A girl there. She was very beautiful and must be of my age with curly blond hair and hazel eyes. I met her near the lake in the evening when I went there to feed the ducks some bread crumbs. We sat near the lake, she was a very shy person, I wanted to be friends with her but she was so shy that she didn't speak a single word, despite her replying to me she was staring at the lake so i sat with her and tried to talk to her but i failed. I was very confused as to why she was not talking to me then I thought maybe I am new to this place so she might be shy to talk to a stranger.

My mom called me for dinner so I got up and said goodbye to her and left the place and ran towards our house. Mom told me to wash my hands and face and come to the dinning room for dinner, so I did what she told me to do and quickly washed my face and hands and sat on the chair of the dining room.

The table was full with all the delicious food. Anna cooked everything for us, she was serving us dinner and we were having the conversation. Mom asked me about the place whether I liked it or not to which I told her I loved it and I even made a new friend here. To which she asked "A new friend! Who is she? I would love to meet your new friend." To which i told her that i met a girl of my age near the lake but i don't know her name to which my mum asked how come she is your friend when you don't know her name. I told her that I tried talking to her but she was not saying anything and she was only looking at the lake. I thought she must be shy to talk to a stranger. To which Anna suddenly cut us in between and asked mom if she can leave early as she got something very important work to do.

Mom nodded her head and she left the house in a hurry. It was very strange for us but we let go and continued our conversation. Dad said " So what were you telling us about your new friend?" I told dad that she didn't talk to me despite my several attempts to talk to her. She was continually looking at the lake. Dad told me to try again. I hope this time she will talk and suggest that I share my toys that will help me to be friends with her. I thanked my dad for this amazing idea and hoped that this will work so that i can be friend her till the time we stay cause frankly speaking there was nothing much to do cause i hardly see people there as the locals were staying far from that place so seeing a kid of my age was the single hope for me to pass my time there, so I desperately wanted her to be my friend.

The next day I glued my eyes near the lake so that I could meet her and be friends with her but she was nowhere to be seen. Anna noticed me and she told me not to go near the lake as it is dangerous but being a kid you do opposite to what is being told you to not do. So I didn't paid much attention to her because i know i was there whole day yesterday and i don't see any red flags and being in a home for whole day is bit boring so i choose to wait for the girl to come so that we can play and i choose a doll from my toys to give it to her as dad told me that this will help me to make her my friend. I slept while waiting for her and when I woke up I ran towards our front door to see if she was there. To my surprise it was evening and she was sitting on the same spot where we were sitting yesterday and she was again looking at the lake.

I took the doll with me and ran towards the lake. She was sitting there but to my surprise she was wearing the same outfit but I ignored the fact and I sat next to her and kept the doll in front of her and asked her "Did you like it? This is for you. Would you like to be my friend?" But she didn't answer any of my questions. I was getting annoyed now by her gesture so I shook her hand and asked her "what's wrong with you?" To which she turned and looked into my eyes, I was scared by now and suddenly she grabbed my arm, it was hurting me. Her grip was so strong. I told her to leave me as it was hurting me, her grip was so strong i could feel the cold hands and being a little kid how can her grip be that strong. I started screaming for help and begging her to leave me but she didn't leave my arm.

I was screaming in pain then i saw Anna coming towards me running and my vision was getting blurred and i felt like i was out of breath, my chest felt so heavy and i fainted. When I came into my senses i saw myself in my room and everybody was sitting near me and they all were looking worried. Mom asked me what happened to me to which i narrated everything which happened to me me but Anna told a shocking fact that when she saw me screaming i was sitting alone but how come it be possible because as far as I remember i was sitting with the girl and she grabbed my arm when it hurts then only i screamed out of pain because she was not leaving me.

Mom Also told me that she also saw me when Anna ran to help me. I was sitting by myself but I was so sure that I was sitting with the girl. I told them that I screamed because the girl was hurting me and I showed them the marks on my hand too. Anna was shocked and my mom was annoyed and asked Anna if she knew about the girl and where she lived so that she could complain to her family about the incident. To which Anna asked my mum if she could talk to her in private to which mom nodded her head and Anna left the room.

Mom told me to take a rest and she left the room.

I wanted to hear what Anna wanted to tell mom so when mom left the room I quietly got up from the bed and listened to their conversation.

I heard Anna told mom that she knows who the girl is to which mom asked "Who is she and where is her home? Tell me Anna."

Anna told my mom "Her name is Rosy! Rosy Victor. She was the daughter of this house's prior owner. Her Mom and and Dad were not in good terms and being the only child their parents were so into fights that they never paid attention to Rosy and When her parents had fight Rosy like to sit near the lake as she felt so lonely as there is nobody to listen to her or give her affection and love which this poor little girl needed the most. One day we heard that while her parents were fighting they didn't paid the attention to the girl and like always she was sitting near the lake and god know how she fell in the lake, when she didn't came for the dinner her mom searched her everywhere but she couldn't able to find her, she they searched her everywhere but they left searching the lake as it was dark, they searched her till morning and finally found her body in the lake.

She was dead due to drowning. Poor girl lost her life because of two irresponsible adults who were so into their egos that they never paid attention to the little girl and she lost her life. Rosy's parents sold the property and left the town and never came back."

Mom asked her "Why did she harm Peace then?"

To which Anna said "I don't know Madam but I know a person who can help you with this. We have a psychic medium in our town and she can see and talk to dead people. She can help us to know about this. We should meet her once."

Mom, Anna and I went to meet Miss Hannah who was a psychic medium in the town. When we reached her house I was so mesmerized by her house decorations, she had an amazing collection of antiques and her house smelled good with all the aromas of different herbs and sage. She had a collection of different gems and stones which she had showcased in her house. She welcomed us with her open heart and suddenly she held my hand and squeezed her eyes and suddenly took a step back. She asked me " When did it start?"
I asked her "what?"

She asked again "When did it start ? When did you start seeing people from the other world?"
I told her everything to which she told us to sit down and she looked at my mother and asked "Is there any near to death experience that happened with this girl?"
To which mom was out of words and kept quiet. She asked again, " Is there any?"
Mom blinked her eyes and I could see her eyes were filled up with tears.
Miss Hannah asked me "Hey! Would you like to see my pet rabbits"
To which I replied "Can I?"
She replied " Yes Of Course."

She told Anna to take me to her garden and let me see her Rabbits by the time she will have a quick chat with my Mom.

Anna took me to the garden and there was a caged room where Miss Anna had her rabbits. I was so excited to see rabbits that I opened their room and started cuddling with them.
Miss Hannah asked my mom "Can you please tell me what it was because I saw a glimpse of a hospital bed and all I could hear was the beeping voice of the hospital machines."

To which Mom replied, " Year back Peace was admitted in the hospital. She was having a high fever, and it was so high that her whole body was shivering badly. We took her to the hospital. Many examinations were done on her but her condition was getting worse day by day. There was not a single test left which was not done over her but her reports were all normal and doctors were shocked about her condition.

When they were done with every examination and her condition was getting worse day by day, doctors told us that there was no chance of survival for her because they failed to get into the roots of the disease. Her body is weak by now and no medication is working on her. And they told us that they can't do anything now. To which Me and
David was so shattered that we started crying outside the Peace's hospital room.

The Nurse was out running and was looking for the doctor and everything was happening so fast that we were unable to guess what was happening with our daughter. We saw from the window of her room that she was surrounded by the team of doctors and everything was in a panic. Around half an hour we got news from the doctor that Peace went into Coma. It felt like the whole world went upside down to us and me and David froze there.

Our daughter was into Coma and she was on a ventilator. Doctor told us that they don't know how long she's gonna survive. Everyone was praying for Peace's recovery. She was in Coma for 12 days and when we lost all the hopes Doctor Brandon came as a ray of hope for us. We were crying for our daughter outside her room and he came all across from Russia on a visit to the Doctor's conference which was held in the same hospital. He noticed us and called us and asked what happened to our daughter. We told him everything to which he asked if he could see Peace's report and upon seeing the report he asked Doctor Lee if he could look into Peace's case and Doctor Lee handed him the case. He examined Peace and asked us to arrange two vaccinations as soon as possible.

The vaccinations were so costly that we had to sell out property because we had invested everything in the hospital and we only left with the house so we sold it and arranged the vaccination and on the thirteenth day Peace came out of coma. We don't know how it happened and what miracle Doctor Brandon did but our child was back to alive.

Once Peace was recovered we purchased the new house which was comparatively smaller but we wanted to restart our lives again but there she encountered the spirit of a lady which was murdered there and with the help of her police solved the case. We sold that house too just to secure our child so that she will not get into any trouble again and we bought this house here in this town but here she also encountered something which I can't explain and we came to you to get the answers."

Miss Hanna consoled my mother and told her that she will help us. Anna brought me inside and Miss Hanna made me sit in front of her and she held my both hands and told me to close my eyes and I did what she said. After a couple of minutes she took a charm and a chain from her drawer that was kept in the box in red velvet cloth. She told me to keep it with me till the right time comes.

Miss Hanna told my mom to take her to the place where we encountered the spirit of a little girl. We reached the lake where she sat and summoned the spirit of the little girl and helped her by making her realize that she was stuck in the loop and ordered her to walk into the way of the bright white light.

She was gone and the air felt so lighter there. Miss Hanna told me "Do you know that you are special Peace? You got a second chance and God chose you to be his messenger. You are blessed with the Third Eye my dear from which you could see the other world and help these poor souls to reach the white light. God has written your destiny and you have to help these souls that are struck in the middle of these two worlds.

It's not easy. You might have to sacrifice a lot and have to make difficult choices in your life. I know you are too young to understand what I am telling you. Don't forget you are blessed by the mighty God and as i said always keep this pendant with you till you."

She gave me a peck on the forehead and she walked towards my mom. She told her " I know it's difficult for you but don't worry the pendant will help her to repress her powers until she is Sixteen after that she has to evoke her powers again and her real life journey will continue from there but make sure she will use her power wisely."
To which mom assured her about the same.

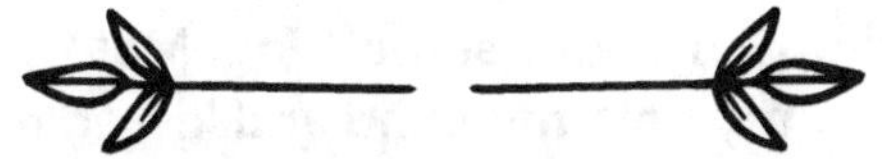

Time passes by and the right time comes where I have started evoking my powers to run wild on the journey of life which destiny has designed for me. 9 years later on my sixteenth birthday mom and Dad came to me and I could see in their eyes that they were worried about something. Mom and dad sat next to me and mom gently held my hand and kissed my forehead and told me "My little princess is grown up now.

Look at my young lady! Peace, we are so blessed to have a daughter like you. We would like to tell you something, I hope you remember Miss Hanna?."
To which I told mom "Of Course mom! How can I forget her? I still remember what she told me about……." I took a long pause and mom squeezed my hands and Dad said " We are proud of you my love and remember we are with you and together we will get through this."

To which i replied " thanks dad but remember Miss Hanna told me that i have to fight this alone and I can't risk any of you and don't worry your princess is strong enough." It was easy to say that "I am strong enough" but deep down I was scared by the unaware situations which I could face in the future. I hugged mom and Dad and I asked mum if i could still keep that pendant with me to which mum agreed. Everything went smoothly and a couple of months passed by and I finished high school too.

Me, Sarah and Mason were besties and we decided that before our college life starts we should have a trip. I remember we had a long discussion on the places where we can go but after a pointless discussion we ended up booking a cottage which was seven hours away from our place. So we decided that it will be great fun, we will have a road trip and the cottage is in isolation and it's an old 19th century house. It's more than what we can expect.

Mason came to pick us up the very next day and our trip started. The whole way we were talking about random stuff and jamming on our favorite songs we finally reached our destination. We came out of the car and saw an old 19th century cottage in front of us. It was looking so royal and beautiful more than what we saw in the picture.

We three were super excited to explore the place. Mr.. Jonathan was waiting for us in front of the cottage door and he greeted us and showed us our rooms. We freshen up quickly and gather in the dining room as it was dinner time.

We had our dinner and then Mr.. Jonathan gave us a quick tour of the house. The house was very beautiful. The walls were filled with the family photographs of Mr.. Hilton who was the owner of the cottage. There was a very beautiful portrait of a lady hanging in the hall of that cottage and I don't know why I couldn't keep my eyes off that picture. It seems that the picture is attracting me towards it and I can't resist myself. It was a good 15 mins that I glued my eyes on that picture, then suddenly Sarah shook me and asked me if I was fine. To which I nodded at her and then I asked Mr.. Jonathan "Hey! Mr.. Jonathan, Who is she in the portrait?"

To which Mr.. Jonathan replied "She is Miss Maria Hilton. Daughter of Mr.. Danis Hilton."
Mason replied "She is gorgeous."
Mr.. Jonathan replied "Indeed! She was."
I asked " What do you mean by "she was"?
Mr.. Jonathan replied " Enough for today, i think you guys should sleep it's late now. I will take a leave and if you guys need anything you can ask me. I am in my room which is next to the hallway. Good night everyone." And Mr.. Jonathan left. We three looked into each other and gave each other a confused look to which Mason replied "Beer any one!"

Sarah replied "I am in!"

And they both pulled my arms and we went to Mason's room and enjoyed our gossip session over chilled beers and called the day off.

The next morning I woke up and got ready for the walk but somehow I wasn't able to take the portrait out of my mind. i want to know more about Her and while getting ready i was sitting in front of the dresser and i saw on the right bottom of the dresser table it was engraved "Marie" and i run my fingers over the engraved alphabets and suddenly i felt a cold breeze over my fave and i don't know how my eyes got closed and I suddenly went into a dream where i saw A young lady must be in her initial twenties sitting on the chair in front of the dresser and Humming a melody and combing her hair, she was so pretty that no words could describe her innocent face. She was the same girl which I saw in the portrait "Maria".

She stood up and went towards the room's window and was looking outside the window as if she was waiting for someone. Soon after a young boy came with his bicycle and waved to her to which she smiled and waved him back from the window and ran downstairs and they held each other's hand and left the house. All of the sudden I felt like someone shocked me and I gained my senses again and I woke up from the dream and it was Sarah who was trying to wake me up. She gave me a glass of water and asked me if I was alright. To which i replied "Sarah i saw something" to which Sarah asked " What is it?"

I showed her the engraved initials on the dresser table and told her " See! "MARIA" is the one who's portrait we saw last night. I think this is her room and i got a vision of her.``
Sarah asked, "What did you see?"

I told her everything to which we decided that we should find out more about Maria's past. By the time Mason was standing outside the door and he saw that we were worried, he asked us about the matter to which Sarah told him everything. Being my besties they know that I am blessed with a super power but it will evoke in such a way we never thought of.

We went downstairs and decided to ask if Mr... Jonathan knew more about Maria but to our surprise we got to know from the cook that Mr... Jonthan is gone out for some work and he will be back home in the evening. We decided to explore the place and asked the cook if he knew anything about this place. To which he said he doesn't know much about the place but there is some family stuff which is kept in the basement but it's always locked and only Mr... Jonathan can access the place as he got the keys but it's been ages he never opened that place.

I asked the cook if he could take me to the basement door to which he agreed and showed us the way. We were standing in front of the door and I slowly kept my hand on the door and within a fraction of second I felt that my hand was being sucked up by some unnatural force and I was into dreams again. I saw Maria was crying and Mr.. Hiltan was scolding her as she had done something wrong.

She was begging to her dad but Mr... Hilton was in extreme rage that he was not listening to her and he ordered a man to lock her daughter in her room to which the man was dragging her and Maria was still crying and begging her dad and Mr.. Holton left the place in anger and Maria was locked in her room and the place went into darkness and I gained my senses again. I told everything which I saw to which Mason and Sarah decided that we should leave this place. They were scared and so was I.

We went to our room and started packing our stuff. Mason got his room on the ground floor and Sarah and I got rooms on the first floor. So we planned that once we are done with packing our stuff we will all gather in Mason's room and leave once Mr.. Jonathan is back home. While I was packing my stuff I felt like someone was watching me, I ignored the fact and continued my packing then all of a sudden I felt like someone grabbed my hand.

It was a cold yet a strong grip and I saw a pale hand holding my wrist. I was scared to death when I looked up and to my shock there was Maria who was holding my wrist. When I looked at her I could feel sadness. My chest was feeling so heavy, the whole vibe of the room turned gloomy and I could see her sad face and tears were rolling from her eyes as if she wanted to tell me.

At that moment I recalled what Miss Hannah told me and I knew at that moment that this is what I meant for, this is why I am blessed with the power of my third eye to help these poor souls to end their sufferings. I knew she wanted my help and I made up my mind that without helping her I wouldn't be leaving this house.

I asked her "Marie, I am not here to harm you in any way. If you need my help give me a sign so that I can help you. I know you are suffering, show me a way so that I can help you."

To which she pointed her finger at a porcelain showpiece. Suddenly the door knocked and she vanished. It was Sarah, she was there with her luggage and she asked me if I was ready to leave. To which i told her "We are not leaving! Call Mason upstairs. I want to talk to you guys." Sarah called Mason in the room and I told them what I saw and how the soul of Marie pointed fingers on that porcelain showpiece.

I told them "Guys! I know this is dangerous and as you know my existence has a motive of helping these souls and I don't want to risk your lives. I want to help Marie but I can't put you guys in danger. It's my destiny and I have to face it alone so you guys can go. I have to help Marie and I promise I will be back soon but you guys have to leave." To which Sarah replied " Are you mad or what? We are not leaving you here on your own." Mason added "We are best friends forever and we ain't going to leave you here. We will face it together." Sarah added "who needs a group hug?"

I know it sounds a bit dramatic but finding such friends are priceless and as it says a great friend will always be in your thick

and thin and here Sarah and Mason proved it and I'm glad that my destiny gave me such superb and priceless gems. We had a group hug and then Mason said "Enough man! You girls are so full of drama. Let's get into the work, girls."
Sarah and I smiled and then I picked up the porcelain showpiece. It was a couple figure but why Marie showed me this?

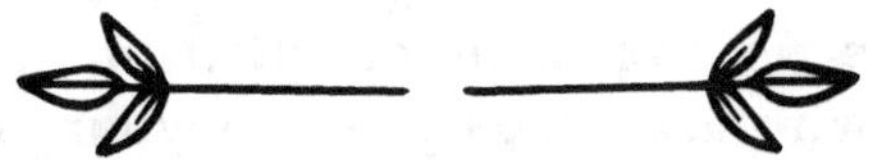

7

I inspected the whole figure but could not find out the clue. Why Marie showed me this and what is in that she needs me to help her with ? There were so many questions in my mind. I asked Sarah and Mason if they could connect anything with this figure. They were totally confused like me. All of the sudden Mason said "Hey! There could be a possibility that she might have hidden something inside it."

We tried to shake the figure but there was no way that one could have stored something in the figure. While shaking I noticed something and I screamed "Hey look! I found it." to which Sarah replied "Chills babes! We are here only to hold your horses please."

I pointed beneath the showpiece. It was engraved Peter then there was a heart drawn and then Maria was written. I connected everything and now I know that Maria wants to know about Peter. That's why her soul is stuck in this world. I told this to Sarah and Mason to which Mason replied "We need to find Peter." Sarah replied "But how? We don't know if he is also alive or not and if he is alive we don't know if he is in this same country or not." Mason added "And if he is alive he must be in his 70's or 80's God knows."

I told them "Only Mr.. Jonathan can answer us because I saw in my vision that Mr.. Jonathan was present there in the basement when Mr.. Hiltan was bashing Maria over something and he himself dragged Maria and locked her in this room whereas Mr.. Helton left the room in rage."

We waited for Mr.. Jonathan and In the evening he came back

from his work. We were sitting in the hall when Mr.. Jonathan came. He greeted us and went inside his room. Here we three were planning how we were gonna make Mr.. Jonathan tells us the truth. After an hour Mr.. Jonathan met us at the dinner table. We had our dinner and after the dinner we asked Mr.. Jonathan if he could sit with us for sometime as we wanted to know more about this place as we have only two days left for our trip and we would love to know the history of this place.

To which Mr.. Jonathan agreed. To which we asked him all the random questions first, he answered every single question and all of the sudden I asked " Mr.. Jonathan tell us about Peter? Who is he?"
To which Mr.. Jonathan's face became pale and his expressions faded away. He replied "I think we need to sleep children. It's too late now and I am tired now. It's been a long day for me."
Mason replied "You can't run away with the questions every time."
Mr.. Jonathan replied "I don't know any Peter and who told you about Peter. Stop it and you guys really need to mind your own business."

We can see anger in Mr.. Jonathan's eyes. As if he wants to hide the truth under his anger.
I replied " We are minding our business just like Peter and Maria were minding their own. Don't you think you did wrong to her. She is still looking for the answer and her soul is still suffering and asking for the closure which you never gave her. You and Me.. Hilton are the ones, because your poor soul is suffering. Why don't you tell us the truth? We want to help her. She asked me to help her."

Suddenly Mr.. Jonathan's expressions again changed and he was filled with guilt and sorrowness.
He replied " Pppppppp Peter!"
Sarah replied "You can tell us Mr.. Jonathan, we really want to help Maria."

Mr.. Jonathan took a deep breath and replied " Peter came here when his father died. His father "Ben" worked here as a gardener. Peter used to come here along with Ben when he was a kid. He used to help his dad and in free time as Maria and Peter were both of the same age they used to play in the garden. Maria didn't have any friends here and when she was too young her mother also passed away. She used to be a traumatic child but the time she met with Peter she became a normal kid again.

Mr.. Hilton saw these changes in her and he was happy with her daughter's progress. Soon they become inseparable and Mr.. Hilton becomes worried about her daughter's obsession. Mr.. Hilton called Ben and told him to send Peter out for studies. He assured Ben that Peter can learn new techniques about farming and gardening and how this will give him a better future. Mr.. Hilton was doing this only to help Maria get out her obsession with Peter but he doesn't know that these two kids now became inseparable. Ben sent Peter out of town for the studies and before leaving the town Peter gifted a porcelain figure to Maria and told her to wait for him, he will be back soon.

It was a long wait of 3 years. Mr.. Hilton thought keeping them away from each other would be a great idea to overcome her daughter's obsession but it showed the negative effects. Maria becomes more defensive and she waits for Peter in the garden and repetitively asks Mr.. Ben about him. After a long wait, finally it was the day when Peter was coming back. Ben told this to Maria and she was excited to meet Peter after a long time. She was waiting restlessly in her room and finally her wait was over.

Peter showed up with his new bicycle and Maria ran to greet him and they spent the whole day with each other. They were often seen together in the town and people were noticing them and it was a hot topic back then that a businessman's daughter is dating a son of his gardener. Soon Mr.. Hilton got to know about their love affair. He called Maria in his office and confronted her.

Maria begged her dad but Mr.. Hilton was so angry that he told Maria that if she will not stop meeting this guy he will put him behind the bars but Maria was so madly in love with Peter that she kept on begging to her dad but Mr.. Hilton ordered me to lock her up in her room and he left the house to see Peter.

Mr.. Hilton confronted Peter also that day and told him to stay away from her because he is not capable of giving Maria a good life. He told Peter that he is not financially stable and how he could support Maria and if he is still gonna see each other then he will put him and his father Ben behind the bars. Peter was a nice guy.

He also thought that he is not stable yet and because of him Maria is gonna sacrifice a lot and he will never be able to give Maria a life which she is currently living. Here Maria was not eating anything; she only demanded her father to see Peter one last time. Maria's health was getting affected day by day because of this and after a month of fighting for her love she left this world."

We could see a grief in Mr.. Jonathan's eyes.
Sarah asked "I'm sorry for your loss Mr.. Jonathan but is there any chance we can meet Mr.. Peter?"
I added "Yes! Mr.. Jonathan Maria is still here with us, I saw her, I saw her in pain and grief. She is still looking for closure. Is there any way we could get connected with Mr.. Peter. Maria's last wish was to see Peter once and that is why her soul is still stuck in this place and she is suffering."

To which Mr.. Jonathan responded "After Ben passed away Peter left this town and I don't have any clue where he is right now but every month end he comes here to visit his Dad's farm."
Mason added "Months end! but today is the day we have to go and check if he is still there, otherwise it will be too late for us."
Mr.. Jonathan replied "but it's too late right now."
Mason replied " we have to rush Mr.. Jonathan, we have to take this chance. Peace you and Sarah should stay here , I will take

Mr.. Jonathan with me and if we are lucky enough we will bring Mr.. Peter here."

And both Mason and Mr.. Jonathan left the house and went to Mr.. Ben's house and luckily Peter was there. Mr.. Jonathan told everything to Peter and they brought Peter back with them.
The moment Peter entered the house he looked everywhere and he burst into tears. He sat on his knees and poured his heart out in front of Maria's portrait. Mr.. Jonathan put his hand on his shoulder and consoled him.

Peter was talking to Maria's portrait and he said " I know I am a coward, I wish I would have fought for us. I just wanted you to be happy but I forgot that your real happiness was with me. I did this because I knew I would never be able to give you comfort but I didn't know that I was going to lose you forever. M sorry Maria and I love You. You were the one for me and ever since you left I never had any other woman in my life. We couldn't meet in this life but I hope we will meet in the other world and then no one can separate us."

I saw Maria standing in the corner and she was looking at Peter. I told Everyone "She is here."
Peter replied "where?"
I pointed my finger towards the hallway. And said "She is standing there and watching us."
Peter said "Maria I am sorry."

And I could see Maria was also grieving. I told her " I know Maria, you never had your closure, you wish to meet Peter last time made you stuck here in this world but now you have to leave this world and you have to move towards the white light." To which Maria came towards me and at this point i was very scared because i never had such encounter before and I didn't know what i have to do next and i froze there but to my surprise Maria hold my wrist again and the moment she touched me i got a vision in which I saw that Maria and i were standing in a empty room and there was a dim light in the room and Maria was standing in front of me.

She put her hand over my hand and said " Am glad you came here and i would like you to tell my Dad that i still love him and tell Mr.. Jonathan that he is an amazing man. And before I leave I would like to thank you for everything. Please give that idol to Peter and tell him I love him. I can see the light and now I can be at peace."
With that she disappeared.

I came out of it and took a deep breath and as she told me to do, I did that. I handed Mr.. Peter the porcelain lady and man figure and told him what Maria told me to tell him and with that I told Mr.. Jonathan what Maria told me to say to him and his dad.

It was a roller coaster ride of emotions that everyone felt in that room but we were happy that finally she is at peace.
We stayed there for two more days and that is how our vacations came to an end but we left that place with lots of memories.

By these retrospective events I felt like I have a preamble to obviate the spirits of the people who are looking for the closures or stuck in this world and seeking peace. But the future held a darker side for me, it changed my whole life and shattered me to the core.

Everything was going smoothly and it's been the past 2 years, there were few activities which i felt but those were not egregious events.

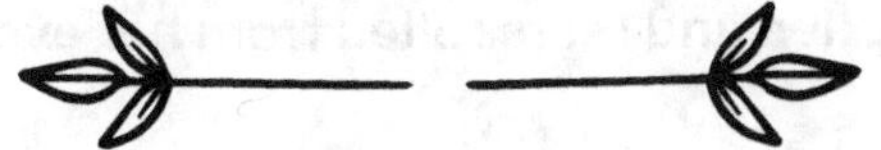

8

After I graduated, I decided to work as a child psychologist and decided to move out of my parents home. I got an opportunity to work with a child care home as a "Child Psychologist". I was very happy but a bit nervous too.

Later that night, i was packing my stuff because in two days i was leaving my parents house and there was so much going on in my mind. My heart was throbbing so fast and my mind was full of "But, If, What and so many other questions." All of the sudden I heard the door knock, It was my Mom.

"Can I come in ?" - Mom asked.

"Mom! You don't need no permission for that. Of course You can." - I replied while stuffing my luggage bag.

"Do you need any help Princess?" - Mom asked and sat next to me and she gently put her hand on my shoulder.

I looked at her and gave her a smile and told her that I am good and she should not worry about anything.

Mom put her hands on my hands and looked at me with concern.

"Mom! Are you alright?" - i asked

"I Don't know baby! A part of me wants you to hold you back from letting you move out but a part of me is very proud of my princess that she is living her dreams and finally flying out of the nest." - Mom replied and tears rolled from her eyes.

"I'm Going to miss you too Mom. I am just a few miles away so don't worry I will be back home every weekend."- I replied to her and hugged mom.

"So can we block this Deal?" - Dad replied.

I looked behind and it was Dad who was listening to our

conversation from outside of my room's door.
" Seal the Deal." - in a chuckling voice I replied.
Mom and dad were my biggest support and without them I wouldn't be able to imagine my life.

Before leaving the town I decided to meet Sarah and Mason so I texted them to meet me the next day so that I could surprise them with the news of me leaving the town and joining the child care home. I don't know how they will take the news, with these thoughts I called the day off.

As decided, we have to meet at our favorite cafe. I reached the place and waited for them. While I was waiting I saw an old gypsy lady sitting opposite to my table and she was continuously looking at me. I was feeling a bit uneasy by the way she was looking at me but I had no other choice because the cafe was full and there were no tables left so that I could switch with. I saw Sarah so I waved to her and she came to the table.

"Where is Mason?" - I asked Sarah.
"He said he will be here in 15 mins and told me to order his favorite Club Sandwich." - Sarah replied.
To which we both replied - " Club Sandwich With Extra Extra Cheeeeeeeeeeeeeeeeez!" and laughed it off.

Mason also joined us and we were talking and I totally forgot about the Lady who was staring at me so out of curiosity i looked at her table to my shock she was still staring at us and when i looked at her she passed a wicked smile, i looked away from her. I don't know but there is definitely something wrong with the lady. I could feel a dark aura around her and I don't know if it's normal or not but I felt like puking and I was feeling dizzy and heavy in my chest. My hands were shaking and I grabbed the glass of water and drank it.

Sarah noticed it and she put her hand on mine and asked me - "Are you Alright?"
To which I nodded her with a yes!

What's wrong with this old lady?" - Mason slammed the table furiously.

"Who?" - Sarah asked.

"This lady who is sitting next to our table, why is she staring at us and passing this weird smile man!" - Mason replied.

"She must be into you, my boy. At Least someone is giving you attention. Enjoy it!" - Sarah replied and winked at Mason and started laughing.

Mason- "Whatever."

I replied - " She has been doing this since I got here. I Don't know how to explain to you guys but am not getting good vibes from her."

"Calm down! Let's take Mason's order and leave this place." - Sarah replied

"Oh yes! Let's go to the Lake and sit there and talk. What do you say?" - Mason replied.

We agreed upon the same. 15 min past by and then the old lady got up from her chair and started coming toward our table. My heart was pounding so bad with each step of her. She came to me and mumbled something in Spanish.

"Cuidado con el fuego. La conocerás pronto." - And she walked away mumbling these words.

"What did she say?" Sarah Asked. Out of us three only Mason knows Spanish.

Mason Replied - " Peace! She told you to "Beware of the fire" and then she said " You will Meet her soon". I don't know if she is talking about her or someone else to meet but she warns you from the fire. Such a weirdo."

I felt like I was out of breath and I just wanted to breathe so I told Sarah and Mason to take me out of this place, I can't take this anymore. We left the cafe and headed towards the lake. Upon reaching the Lake we decided on a place to sit down. I caught my breath but on the back of my mind the thought of the gypsy lady was haunting me. Mason's and Sarah's placatory words gave me strength to take those thoughts out of my mind. I told them that I am leaving the town tomorrow as I got a job in a child care home. There was an utter silence between us three.

"Congratulations!" - Mason replied.
"We are going to miss you bestie!" - Sarah added.
"Don't be overdramatic you guys! Chill, I will be visiting home on weekends." - I replied.
We toasted our friendship and relaxed near the lake side while chatting over random stuff.

After getting back home, I started finishing my packing. I went to check on Mom and Dad. I knew they were not showing me their concern but from inside they were distressed about me moving out. Mom was working in the kitchen, I hugged her from the back and placated her that i will be fine in the new place and told her that as i promised i will be coming home on weekends.
"Oh yes! Our princess sealed the deal. Don't you Princess ?" - Dad Replied.
"Yes! Of course Dadda." - I chuckled and hugged Dad.

After finishing our dinner we called off the day. Tomorrow was a big day because I was leaving my house and about to start my new life at a new place. I was feeling like a bird who is about to leave the nest to explore the world.

 I left my place in the morning for the Child Care Home. By the evening I reached there and Mrs. Martha Welcomed me. She took me to her office for further formalities and allotted me a room. I decided that by the time i will not find an apartment near the Foster home i will be staying in the room allotted by Mrs. Martha.

 I was so tired that I collected the keys and headed towards the room allotted to me. The room was pitch dark when I opened it and I started searching for the switches to turn on the light. This was the first time that I was getting an eerie feeling from the darkness. There was a feeling of being claustrophobic, I was looking for the switches in haste. After hustling for a bit finally I found the switches, when I turned on the light I found it was an old Victorian designed room. I looked around and opened the window for the fresh air to come inside the room as it seemed that the room was not in use for a long time. I unpacked my luggage and organized my wardrobe and a few other things and rested a bit.

There was a knock at the door, I got up and peeked through the door's peephole and I asked - "Who is there?"
"Hello Miss Peace, Myself Roushell. I came here to tell you that Mrs. Martha is calling you for dinner. Please follow me because there is a certain time allotted for the dinner and I must hurry up."
I opened the door and greeted Miss Roushell and followed her to the dining room.

There was a huge dining hall for the kids and in the right corner there was a small dining room for the staff. A huge table was placed in the middle of the dining room and the whole place was having a Victorian touch. Mrs. Martha pointed at the chair next to her and introduced me to the staff. The kids had already left the dining room, there was a rule that every kid will have first then only the staff could have their meals and it was strictly served on time. After finishing the dinner Mrs. Martha called me in her office and handed me a file and told me to read it. It was a "Rule Book".

I was about to leave but she called me again and said - "Tomorrow will be your first day and you must be aware that you will be working under Mr.. Louis." I nodded her yes.
She took a deep breath and replied - " Before you leave I would like to tell you something."
I could feel agitation in her voice. She took a long pause and looked me in the eyes and replied -
" I handed you the file of Rules which one should have to follow while working here and I believe that you take this seriously." I assured her by saying - " Yes! Mrs. Davis I will."

I left her office and came back to my room and placed the file on the study and went for a shower. After taking a good dip I felt so rejuvenated. I read the file and kept it inside my side table.

My phone rang and it was my dad calling and we had a good long talk and then I disconnected the call. I saw it was already 9:30 pm and I was so tired because I traveled the same day and then did all the formalities here so I decided to sleep early today so that I could have a fresh start tomorrow morning. I was having a sound sleep but in the middle of the night my door knocked. I woke up to the sound and checked my phone. It was 1:49 am.

I asked myself, who could be there at my door?. Again there was a knocking sound at the door. At this point of time I felt a little weird so I got up to check who it could be but I decided to first check through the peephole. Upon checking I saw nobody was there. So I tucked myself in the bed again and tried sleeping again because I knew that I had a lot of work to do in the morning.

I woke up with a loud noise from my alarm which I set a day before. I searched my phone with my half eyes shut. It was six in the morning so I got up and made my bed and went for a shower. I don't want to get late on my first day at work. I got ready and grabbed all the important documents with me and headed towards Mrs.. Martha's office. Upon reaching her office I knocked on the door gently. Mrs. Martha told me to come in.

A man must be in his thirties, tall and well built with chiseled jawline was already sitting there, upon entering i greeted Mr.. Martha and him. Mr.. Martha Introduced me to this man, he was Mr.. Louis with whom i have to work.
"Meet Mr.. Louise, You will be working under him as a Junior Child psychologist." - Mr.. Martha Replied.
"Hello Miss Peace, It will be a pleasure working with you as a team." - Mr.. Louis reached out for a hand shake with a smile.
"Oh! Hello Mr.. Louis. I've heard a lot about you and It will be a great pleasure for me to work under your guidance." - I replied while shaking hands with Mr.. Louis.
"I hope you only heard good things about me." - Mr.. Louis Replied and chuckled at the same time.
"Now you can take your charge and excuse me. I have something important to finish." Mrs. Martha replied.

Mr.. Louis asked me to follow him to his office. The Office was at the end of the first floor. It was a huge room with big windows to pass the sunlight and the fresh air and there were two working desk placed in the room and a huge bookshelf in one corner and in one corner there was a lockers placed on the walls with the labels on it, where all the data were kept in a systematic way. It Seems Mr.. Louis was very good at his work, everything was kept systematically and neatly in his office. He showed me my desk and asked me to settle down first and then he settled down in his seat. The whole room was filled with his intense cologne fragrance. He called me to his desk and briefed me on the case of a young boy named Rex. He told me to go through with the case study of this young boy and make notes on the same by tomorrow. He handed me his file and I got back to my desk.

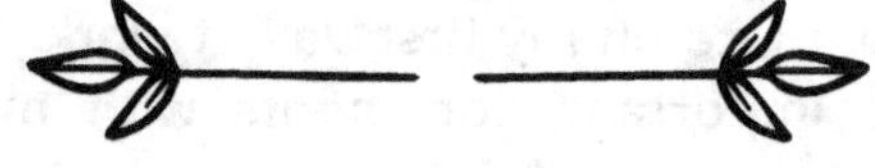

9

I was sitting at my desk and was reading the case of Rex and upon reading I came to the conclusion that it was the case of "Pyromania". An obsessive desire to set fire to things but in his case he was doing it with himself. I raised my eyebrows while reading the case file and got up from my place to which Mr.. Louis asked -

"Are you alright Miss?"

"Yes Mr.. Louis but I figured out something with this case study of Rex." - I replied.

"What is It ?"- Mr.. Louis asked

" If I am not wrong, it's a case of Pyromania. Isn't it ?" - I asked Mr.. Louis

Mr.. Louis took a long pause and replied-

"Yes it is! But I am not able to figure out what trauma triggered this poor kid to do such acts."

"Is there any back history of Rex? I would like to know everything about his past so that it will be easier for us to get to the root cause." - I replied.

"There must be his case file in the records. Rex came to this shelter home a few days back. I guess Mrs. Martha must have his details." - Mr.. Louis replied

"Can I meet this kid?" - I asked.

"Yes of course you can. I must say Mrs. Martha appointed a best candidate for this post. I am impressed." - Mr.. Louis replied.

I decided to talk to Mrs. Martha regarding the case of Rex. I want to know all the major details of Rex's family as well as his medical history. So I headed towards Mrs. Martha's office and knocked on her door, she called me in and offered me to sit.

After having a few discussions I asked her about Rex's family history to which she handed me his file. In the file we can clearly see that Rex was only Nine years old when he was found sitting outside his house in a terrible position while his house was completely burned down and he lost his mother in the accident a year ago. After getting here in the care center he made several attempts to harm himself and fellow roommates by setting up the fire but every time no evidence was found how he started the fire other than that there was no other information recorded in the file.

Strange! Right?
How is this possible for a ten year old kid to start a fire without even leaving any evidence behind and this is actually something strange that my mind was not digesting it, so i decided to meet Rex personally to find more about him.

I was lost in the thoughts of this anomalous case and soon a pleasant smell of a cologne drew my attention. it was familiar, the rich note of wood and amber can be a delight for your nostrils. I regained my consciousness and saw Mr.. Louis standing next to my table. I was stiff with fear and acknowledged him. He gave a smirk and asked me if I was okay or not. I nodded at him in embarrassment and apologized to him. I asked him to be seated as I wanted to discuss the case of Rex. I asked for his permission to talk to Rex personally to which he granted me the permission and told me that he will also join so that he can also monitor him as it will be beneficial for the case study. He said he will notify Mrs. Martha and after that we can proceed. At the end of the day Mr.. Louis told me that we will be meeting Rex after the dinner.

After dinner Mr.. Louis met me in the corridor and told me to follow him to Rex's room. I nodded him and started following him in the passage of the boys wing. Rex's room was at the end of the passage and in a few minutes we were standing in front of his room's door. There was something Dark and heavy. I could feel it in the air and I could feel a sharp pain in my right shoulder. I ignored it but the discomfort can be seen on my face.

"Are you fine Miss?" - Mr.. Louis asked me.
In a stumbling voice I replied to him- " Yes Mr.. Louis, I am fine, it's just my right shoulder suddenly started paining. It must be because of the hectic day other than that I am doing great."
Mr.. Louis smiled and replied- "Doing Great haaah! You are setting my graph of expectation high Miss. So, are you ready to deal with your first Subject?"
"Ready than ever Mr.. Louis." - I replied

Mr.. Louis opened the door and there was a dead silence in the room as only Rex was staying in that room. It's not like he has been kept there intentionally alone but in the past he tried setting things on fire and the Care center's administration doesn't want to risk anyone's lives. Other kids were actually scared of Rex and that is the reason he is staying alone in the room but there was an order by the administration that a staff will be keeping a close eye on the activities of Rex so that he doesn't risk his own life as well.

Rex was sitting on his Bed and upon seeing us he got up and greeted us. It was strange that the kid who was always into him and who doesn't even reply to any of the staff members of the Child care center and kept quite all the time minding his own business actually greeted us that too in a cheerful manner. Mr.. Louis looked at me with a completely blank face as if he was also witnessing him like this for the very first time.

"Hey Champ! How was your day?" - Mr.. Louis asked Rex and stroked his hands on his hair.
Rex looked into the face of Mr.. Louis blankly and hid himself behind me and grabbed me tightly from behind as if he was scared of Mr.. Louis.
I bring him in front of me and gently squeezed his hands and asked him-
"Hey sweety it's fine you don't have to get scared of Mr.. Louis. Can we talk a little bit if it's fine with you ?"
Rex nodded in a yes. I asked him again-
"So tell me what's your favorite color?"
"Green" - He replied

"Oh! So you love Green, Mine is Blue." - Mr.. Louis replied to him in a teasing way.

Rex looked at his face and kept quiet and I could see a look of despair on Mr.. Louis' face.

" Hey, who wants to have Ice Cream?" - I asked to handle the situation

I can see a spark in Rex's eyes and he raised his arm in excitement.

To gain the trust Mr.. Louis also raised his arm and said - "Oh! Great me too."

Let's go out and have Rex's favorite Ice Cream. Who all are coming with me ?" - I asked

"Treat is on me." - Mr.. Louis Replied

Mr.. Louis took permission from Mrs. Martha and we took Rex out for Ice Cream. The whole idea behind this was to make him feel comfortable so that we could actually get to know what this little kid is going through.

We reached to an Ice-cream parlour and Rex order his favorite "Chunky Monkey Ice-cream"

We had a lovely time out there and Rex was also responding to us well. Mr.. Louis was also amazed by seeing him like this for the first time since he came into the child care center. He was a frightened kid and he used to be in himself all the time.

"Good job Peace." - Mr.. Louis looked at me and whispered.

I Smiled and then started asking random questions to Rex. It was very important for us to gain his trust and so far now we are succeeding in it.

Upon returning back to the child care center Rex held my hand and took me back in his room and made me sit on his bed and wanted me to close my eyes until he would not say to open them. I did the same and Mr.. Louis was watching all this while standing on the door of his room. Rex opened his Wardrobe and pulled out a stuffed Dinosaur toy and came back to me and said - "Open your eyes!"

I opened my eyes and I saw a soft toy in his hands. It was a

Green color Dinosaur Plush toy.

"I can see it's your favorite color toy. Isn't it ?" - i asked Rex

He giggled and said - "Yes! Mommy gave me this."

"Oh your Mommy gave this to you. This is so cute just like you sweety." - I replied

All of the sudden he went quiet and I could see his happiness fade while looking at his toy.

"Can I hug you Miss Peace." - Rex asked gently

"Yes of course sweetie. Come here. Are you fine?" - I gave Rex a hug and asked him if he was okay.

"Come on, show me your Dinosaur." - I asked just to divert his mind.

He gave me his plush toy and the moment he put that plush toy on my hand, It felt like a wave of current passed through my whole body and I froze there. A sharp pain again shoots on my Right shoulder and I writhe in pain. Mr.. Louis immediately came towards me and asked me if I'm alright but I could not speak as the pain was immense. I felt like everything stopped and I could not hear anything and everything blacked out for me and then I saw a glimpse of Rex's past. I saw a Lady give that plush toy to Rex and hugged her and told him to leave the house and wait for her on the other side of the house and I could see her right shoulder was bleeding badly as if it was stabbed by some sharp object. I saw her resting as the pain was unbearable for her but suddenly a hand came from behind and it started pulling her from hair and dragging her to the other end and suddenly i could feel tremendous heat all over my body as if someone is burning me in unconscious state i let out howl of pain and i came into senses and i could see Me.. Louis and Rex both were sitting next to me and both were looking at me. I got up and told Mr.. Louis that it's late now and we should get back to our rooms and sleep. Mr.. Louis nodded in a yes and I gave a peck on Rex's forehead and tucked him in his bed and said - " Bye! Good night, Sleep well. Will see you tomorrow champ."

He replied - " Good night Miss Peace. I hope you are fine?"

"She is champ! It's Miss Peace's first day here and she must be tired. Now you Sleep, we will meet you tomorrow." Mr.. Louis

Replied.
While I was about to leave Rex, he held my hand and gesticulated with his other hand to bring my ear near to him and he whispered - "Did you see him?"
" See Who?" - I asked.
"The Bad Man" - He replied.

He was about to speak but suddenly there was a knock on the door and it was the member of the staff who came to check Rex whether he was asleep or not.
Mr.. Louis told me to leave for now as it was late and by this time Rex should have slept. I smiled at Rex and told him to sleep and left the room with Mr.. Louis. Mr.. Louis asked me - "Are you alright?".
I replied - "Yes!'
He again asked - "What happened to you there?"
"Where?" - I replied.
"Don't you know? You froze there holding your shoulder and not responding to us for a good five minutes." - He replied.
I gathered the courage and looked in the eyes of Mr.. Louis and Replied-
"Right now I can not explain to you much. Trust me I will answer your every question but right now it's not the time. Please excuse me. I have to take a leave for now."
After that I left Mr... Louis hung there with a puzzled look.

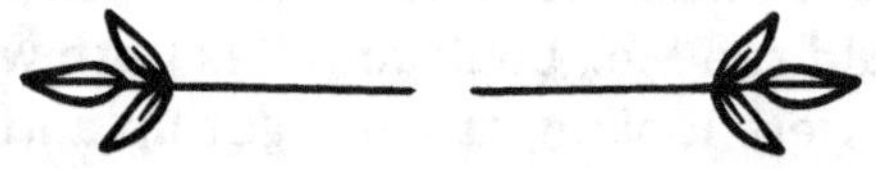

10

Several days went by and it was hard to even face Mr.. Louis, his piercing glaze was something I wasn't able to resist much. I decided to tell Mr.. Louis about the vision I got without being hesitant about what he was going to think about me. It was noon and he was on his desk working and i got up from my desk and went straight to him and told him-
"I need to talk to Mr.. Louis and it's important."

He didn't pay much attention to me and kept on working on his documents. I whacked on the table and my eyes were full of tears and i again said -
"I need to talk to you and I can't hide this anymore."
He stood up from his chair and said -
"Now what?"
"I know you want me to answer your questions and I will answer them all but i don't know how you are going to take it." - I replied

Mr... Louis looked into my eyes and replied - " I noticed your reaction when you touched Rex's toy and after that you acted so abnormal and weird, upon my asking several times you just kept me hanging like insane and I don't deserve this cold behavior. What's wrong with you Peace tell me, why are you acting so strange?"

With a feeling of deep trust in Mr... Louis, I decided to open up about my psychic abilities. I wanted to share everything I saw about Rex and his mother, revealing the dark and painful truth.
"Mr.. Louis I will answer your every question but you have to listen to me very carefully and I want you to trust me." - I replied

To which he nodded his head.
" I am a psychic Medium and I can see what a normal human can't see. I am blessed with psychic powers where I can see the souls and past related to them."
"What? Are you even real? Wait what? What you just said you can see past? Are you joking?" - Mr.. Louis replied

"Am serious Mr... Louis you have to trust me with that and it's not like i can see the past i only can see the past related to the souls. It's like they want to channel me." - I replied.
"Then what did you see when Rex handed you the toy?" - Mr.. Louis replied
"I saw Rex's mother and she was injured, like very badly injured and she escaped Rex from the house and then I saw something strange that a man was dragging him but before I could analyze the situation the channel broke." - I replied.

"Oh yes! I heard that Rex's mother and his mother's boyfriend were in the building when the fire started and the fire was so intense that the body which local police discovered was fully burned. Everyone thought the deaths of both were due to an outbreak of fire due to a gas leak." - Mr.. Louis replied.

I insisted that Mr.. Louis take me to the site where this happened so that we can know more about it. He hesitated first but upon my insisting he agreed.

We reached the location. We saw, In the depths of a desolate land, hidden away from prying eyes, there stood an old burned house that exuded an eerie presence. It was as if the very air around it was tinged with a sense of foreboding. Approaching the house sent a shiver down my spine. The once charming wooden exterior now appeared weathered and burnt. As we cautiously make our way through the charred remains, a sense of unease settles over us. The house stands as a haunting reminder of the past. Its entrance is partially hidden, covered in soot and debris.

The front porch creaked with each step, as if whispering secrets of the past. Inside the house the air was heavy with a musty scent, as if the house had been untouched for centuries. Cobwebs adorned every corner, their delicate threads trembling in the slightest breeze. The living room portraits that once held cherished memories are now half burned and we ventured further into the house, the creaking floorboards echoed with each step, as if the house itself was whispering secrets from its dark past. The kitchen, once a place of nourishment, now felt cold and abandoned and burnt completely .The silence was broken only by the distant sound of dripping water, creating an atmosphere of unease.

Upstairs, the bedrooms were frozen in time, their windows covered by tattered burnt curtains. The beds were unmade, the sheets were burnt and it looks as if their occupants had vanished without a trace. The air grew thicker, as if unseen eyes were watching our every move. This house is in the middle of nowhere, holding a sinister aura that sends chills
With trepidation, I push aside the remnants and ascend the stairs. The air grows heavy, and a chill runs down from my spine. As we climbed the creaky staircase, the air grew heavy with a sense of malevolence. The attic door loomed before us, covered in peeling paint and stains of fire that revealed layers of forgotten history. With a trembling hand, I pushed the door open, revealing a room that seemed frozen in time.

The attic was more like a chamber. The walls were adorned with ancient symbols, etched into the wood with precision. Their meaning was unknown, but their presence sent a shiver down my spine. I looked at Mr. Louis and said - "This is it!"
This is the first time I spoke since we entered this house. I told Mr.. Louis to stay outside the attic room.

In the center of the room, a worn-out wooden table stood as a macabre centerpiece. On its surface lay remnants of sinister rituals, their purpose lost to the ages. Dried bloodstains marred the wood, hinting at the dark practices that had taken place within those walls.

A collection of weathered books lined the shelves, their leather bindings cracked and faded. Their contents were a forbidden knowledge, filled with incantations and spells that should never be uttered. Dust-covered relics and mysterious artifacts adorned the space, each holding a story of its own.

As I cautiously explored the attic, I stumbled upon an old, tattered journal. Its pages were filled with handwritten entries, detailing the twisted experiments and rituals that had once taken place. The words seemed to dance off the pages, whispering secrets that should have remained buried.

It was strange that the whole house was burned but this room and everything inside it was intact as it is. In that attic, the remnants of sinister rituals left an indelible mark. It was a place where darkness thrived and where the line between the living and the dead blurred. It serves as a chilling reminder of the unspeakable horrors that once unfolded within those walls. The air grew colder, and an otherworldly presence seemed to fill the room. Shadows danced along the walls, their movements mocking my presence. The sound of distant whispers echoed in my ears, as if the spirits of the past were still trapped within those walls.

As I investigate further, whispers seem to echo through the air. It's as if the spirits of the past are trying to communicate with me, urging me to uncover their secrets. Feeling a mix of fear and curiosity, I told Mr.. Louis to document the findings and decided to leave the attic, vowing to return another day to uncover the truth behind the sinister rituals that once took place in this eerie place.

Just when we were about to leave the place I stumbled upon an old ledger which had Satan symbols on it. The moment I touched it, a surge of energy coursed through my body and I had a vision again. I froze in time as if some power wanted to reveal the horrifying truth of the sinister act once happened here.
I saw the room was filled with eerie symbols, and a fire burned

in the center and a man was sitting next to it chanting some spells. My heart raced as I realized the ritual involved the same room where I was standing. It was the "Attic". The flames grew higher, and a dark presence filled the room and the man who was performing the ritual suddenly stopped chanting and it felt like everything stopped and suddenly he turned his face towards me. My whole body froze in terror of what I just saw. It was a man with a burnt face, he stood up and charged me with great force. He strangled me so that I wasn't able to breathe. I was struggling for breath, As I gasped for breath, my heart was pounding, I stumbled upon Mr... Louis. He quickly rushed to my side, offering a steady hand. With his support, I regained my composure and caught my breath. Overwhelmed with gratitude, I tightly embraced him, feeling a sense of safety in his arms.

But the moment of solace was short-lived. In a hushed voice, I whispered to him about the looming danger. A dark entity, lurking in the shadows, threatened our lives. Determined to escape its clutches, I implored him to leave the place swiftly.

We locked eyes, our hearts were racing in sync, as we prepared to face the unknown together. With a shared resolve, we set off on a daring escape from that place.

 came into senses and i could see, Mr.. Louis and Rex both were sitting next to me and both were looking at me. I got up and told Mr.. Louis that it's late now and we should get back to our rooms and sleep. Mr.. Louis nodded in a yes and I gave a peck on Rex's forehead and tucked him in his bed and said - " Bye! Good night, Sleep well. Will see you tomorrow champ."
He replied - " Good night Miss Peace. I hope you are fine?"
"She is champ! It's Miss Peace's first day here and she must be tired. Now you Sleep, we will meet you tomorrow." Mr.. Louis Replied.
While I was about to leave Rex, he held my hand and gesticulated with his other hand to bring my ear near to him and he whispered - "Did you see him?"
" See Who?" - I asked.
"The Bad Man" - He replied.

He was about to speak but suddenly there was a knock on the door and it was the member of the staff who came to check Rex whether he was asleep or not.

Mr.. Louis told me to leave for now as it was late and by this time Rex should have slept. I smiled at Rex and told him to sleep and left the room with Mr.. Louis. Mr.. Louis asked me - "Are you alright?".

I replied - "Yes!'

He again asked - "What happened to you there?"

"Where?" - I replied.

"Don't you know? You froze there holding your shoulder and not responding to us for a good five minutes." - He replied.

I gathered the courage and looked in the eyes of Mr.. Louis and Replied-

"Right now I can not explain to you much. Trust me I will answer your every question but right now it's not the time. Please excuse me. I have to take a leave for now."

After that I left Mr... Louis hung there with a puzzled look.

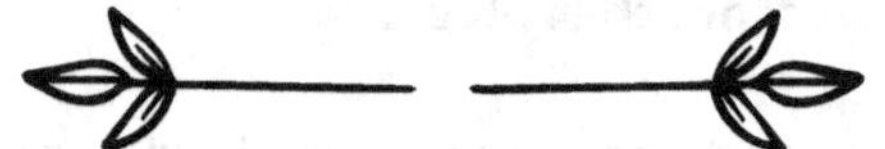

It's been almost a week since we returned from that place. Me and Mr.. Louis had not spoken well from that day about the incident. While working on my desk I opened the drawer of my desk and there was the ledger kept which we found from Rex's mother's house.

I asked Mr... Louis if he kept the ledger here, to which he said yes. I took Rex's dad's ledger in my hand , as my fingers grazed the worn pages of the book she had acquired from that place. Suddenly, a surge of energy coursed , and my mind was filled with vivid images. A psychic vision revealed a desperate ghostly lady, pleading for her help.

The whole atmosphere turned pitch black and an apprentice of a ghostly figure of a lady emerges from the dark . Surprisingly i was not getting any chills from her. It feels the aura of that entity was pure. She came near and told me that she is "Cassandra", mother of Rex. She pleaded with me to save her kid from the clutches of her boyfriend Baxter.
To which I asked her, "How can I help Rex and Who is Baxter?
She pointed her hands towards me and asked me to touch her finger and she channeled her vision to me.

She told me that she and Baxter met in a downtown bar. Baxter was in his low phase and she approached him, they started seeing each other now and then and soon they started dating each other and after a few months of dating Baxter proposed to Cassandra for the marriage. When she was narrating her story to me I could actually channel her visions and I could see how happy they were. Baxter was a struggling Artist in the Music industry. And as a part time he used to sing in Bar where he first met Cassandra.

After they got married Baxter got a call from an agency and he got signed for a stage show that was going to be held soon and there will be a huge crowd involved, to which on getting the show Baxter and Cassandra were so happy. Baxter put his all effort in practicing for her first breakthrough. There Cassandra got to know that she is expecting her first baby and decided to break this news to Baxter after his show. She wanted him to be focused as it was a dream come true for Baxter.

Soon the day came when Baxter had to perform. The stage was lit and everything was looking glam and it was the time when Baxter had to perform. The musicians were ready, and Baxter felt ready too. As the curtain rolled up, revealing a huge crowd, Baxter's heart raced with a mix of nerves and anticipation.

But as the spotlight shone on him, Baxter's stage fright got the best of him. The words that were supposed to flow effortlessly from his lips stumbled and faltered. It was a challenging experience, and the audience's disappointment was palpable. They began to boo and express their frustration.

Feeling crushed by the negative reaction, Baxter made the difficult decision to step away from the stage. It was a really heartbreaking moment for Baxter. The Break he was waiting for so long has slipped out of his hands. For the past few days he kept himself locked in his room, Cassandra tried to talk with him but he was not in his senses the lashback and criticism by the crowd was not letting him Sleep for days. He started taking drugs and became alcoholic and it was the first time when he raised his hand on Cassandra when he threw his bottle on the floor. Cassandra yelled at him that this is not what she deserves and the little one who is still inside him does not deserve this either. Baxter was shocked upon hearing that they are expecting a baby and he grabbed Cassandra in his arms and Cassandra just melted in his arms they both cried and Baxter decided that he will now act more maturely and they will welcome their Son happily and for that he will work hard. He refused to let this setback define his entire music career. But little did he know that his destiny had something else written for him. He tried asking work from different people but he only faced rejection due to that first failed attempt.

Feeling crushed, Baxter was walking on the empty roads and sat on the bridge, his head in his hands, his heart heavy with sadness and disappointment. He had once dreamed of achieving fame and success, but now all he could see was failure and despair. As he sat there, lost in his thoughts, a stranger approached him. The man was tall and imposing, with a mysterious glint in his eye. Baxter looked up, surprised by the sudden presence of the stranger.

"Are you okay?" the man asked, his voice low and soothing.
Baxter shook his head, unable to find the words to express his pain.

The man sat down next to him and placed a hand on his shoulder. "I understand how you feel," he said softly. "I've been where you are, and I know a way to help you achieve the fame and success you desire."

Baxter looked at the man, his curiosity piqued. "How?" he asked, eager for any glimmer of hope.
The man smiled, a strange and unsettling grin. "There is a ritual you can perform," he said. "A ritual that will bring you all the fame and success you could ever dream of. But be warned, it comes at a price."

Baxter felt a shiver run down his spine. "What price?" he asked, his voice barely a whisper.

The man leaned in closer, his eyes burning with intensity. "You must make a deal with the devil," he said. "Sell your first child's soul to Satan, and in return, you will be granted unparalleled fame and success."

.Baxter recoiled in horror. "I could never do that," he said, his voice filled with fear and disbelief.
The man laughed, a cold and chilling sound. "Suit yourself," he said, standing up and preparing to leave. "But know this, the opportunity may never come again."

As Baxter watched the stranger walk away, a seed of doubt and temptation took root in his mind. Could he really achieve his dreams by making a deal with the devil? The thought both terrified and intrigued him.

Days passed, and John found himself consumed by the idea of the ritual. The allure of fame and success pulled at his heart, whispering promises of a better life. Finally, unable to resist any longer, he made his decision.

It had been several days since Baxter had encountered the mysterious stranger on the bridge, but the memory of their unsettling conversation still lingered in his mind. He had tried to push it to the back of his thoughts, but every now and then, he would remember the stranger's chilling words.
One night, as Baxter was walking home from work, he saw the stranger standing at the same spot. His heart skipped a beat as he approached him cautiously.

"Hello again," the stranger said with a sly grin. "I see you haven't forgotten our little conversation."
Baxter felt a chill run down his spine. He couldn't understand why the stranger had reappeared in his life again.

"What do you want from me?" the man asked, his voice trembling with fear.

The stranger chuckled darkly. "I want to offer you a chance at fame and fortune beyond your wildest dreams. All you have to do is follow my instructions."
Baxter's curiosity was piqued, despite his unease. He couldn't

deny that the idea of fame had always appealed to him.

"Tell me what I have to do," he said, trying to keep his voice steady.

The stranger leaned in closer, his eyes glinting with malice. "First, you must seek out a secluded isolated spot in your house. There, you must draw a pentagram on the ground and light five black candles at each point. Then, you must recite the incantation I will provide you with, calling upon the powers of darkness to grant you fame and success."

Baxter listened intently as the stranger outlined the ritual process in detail. Despite his growing apprehension, he couldn't shake the allure of the promise of fame and fortune.

As the stranger finished explaining the ritual, he gave Baxter a piece of paper with the incantation written on it. It involved worshiping Satan for six years, performing dark deeds in his name, and ultimately sacrificing my own child's soul to the devil.

Baxter hesitated for a moment, his mind filled with doubts and fears. But the thought of achieving his dreams was too tempting to resist.
That night, under the cover of darkness, Baxter ventured into the attic of his own house and carried out the ritual as the stranger had instructed. As he recited the incantation, a feeling of dread crept over him, but he pushed it aside, focusing on the promise of success. When he had finished, a strange sensation washed over him, leaving him feeling both exhilarated and unnerved.

In the following days, Baxter began to notice subtle changes in his life. Opportunities seemed to present themselves out of nowhere, and he found himself climbing the ranks of success faster than he could have ever imagined. But with each new triumph, a sense of unease gnawed at him, reminding him of the dark pact he had made.

As his fame grew, Baxter found himself haunted by visions and nightmares, his conscience weighed down by guilt and regret. He realized too late that the price of his success had been his child's soul, sold to the devil in exchange for a fleeting taste of glory.

Months later Cassandra suddenly went into labor. Panicked and excited, they rushed to the hospital, and after a few hours of intense pain, Cassandra gave birth to a healthy baby boy.

As the nurses placed the newborn in Cassandra's arms, Baxter's heart swelled with love and joy. He couldn't believe how perfect his son was, with his tiny fingers and tiny toes, and he couldn't wait to watch him grow and become a man.

But as the hours passed and the adrenaline wore off, a dark thought began to creep into Baxter's mind. He remembered the pact he had made with Satan months ago in exchange for success and fortune. Part of that pact was that he would sacrifice his firstborn child to the devil.

Baxter was horrified by the thought, but he couldn't shake the feeling that he had made a promise that he now had to fulfill. He tried to push the thought away, to focus on the miracle of his son's birth, but the guilt gnawed at him.

For five long years, Baxter participated in these rituals, sacrificing his morals and humanity in the process. He could feel himself changing, his once warm heart turning cold and callous. As the rituals continued, Baxter's appearance began to transform as well newfound powers and charisma drew others in, and he soon found himself becoming a popular independent singer. His dark, haunting melodies captivated audiences, and his cold-hearted aura only seemed to add to his mystique.

It was a quiet evening as Cassandra walked upstairs to grab a book from the attic, she heard faint chanting coming from above. Curious, she pushed open the attic door and was shocked to find Baxter standing in the center of a circle of candles, a book of dark magic open in front of him.

Cassandra's heart raced as she watched in horror as Baxter continued his sinister rituals. She never knew he had an interest in the occult, but she never imagined he would be involved in something so dark and twisted. Fear crept up her spine as she slowly backed away, careful not to make a sound.
As soon as Baxter finished his ritual and left the attic, Cassandra Decided to check the attic and stumbled upon something that made her heart skip a beat. Hidden in the corner of the attic, tucked away behind old blankets and forgotten clothes, was a small, leather-bound book with a cryptic symbol etched on its cover.

Curiosity piqued, Cassandra opened the book and felt a chill run down her spine as she read the words inscribed on its yellowed pages. It was a pact, a pact signed in blood, a pact between her husband and the devil himself.

Her hands trembled as she read the details of the deal - her husband had sold their son's soul to Satan in exchange for wealth and power. Tears streamed down her face as she realized the extent of the betrayal, the depth of the deception.

Heartbroken and devastated, Cassandra fell to her knees, clutching the cursed book in her hands. How could her husband, the man she had loved and trusted for so many years, do such a thing? How could he sacrifice their own flesh and blood for his own selfish desires?

Cassandra knew she had to leave. She didn't want to be anywhere near her husband if he was involved in something so sinister. Tears welled up in her eyes as she quickly packed a bag and made her way out of the house with rex.

In that moment, Cassandra's world shattered. The love she had once felt for her husband turned to ash, replaced by a searing anger and grief that threatened to consume her whole. She knew what she had to do.

As the sun began to set, Cassandra grabbed Rex by the arm and quietly slipped out of the house. She knew her husband would be furious, but she couldn't bear to see her son suffer.

Just as they reached the end of the driveway, Cassandra heard the sound of heavy footsteps behind her. She turned around to see her husband, red-faced and angry, running towards them.

Inside the house, Cassandra's husband unleashed a barrage of insults and threats, demanding to know where she thought she was going. Tears streamed down Cassandra's face as she pleaded with him to let her leave, but he was deaf to her cries.

Before she could react, he grabbed her by the arm and forcefully dragged her back into the house. Rex tried to intervene, but his father's grip was too strong.

With a heavy heart, Cassandra confronted Baxter, her voice shaking with emotion as she told him the damning evidence she had unearthed in the attic. Baxter's eyes widened in shock and fear as he realized that his dark secret had been exposed.

"So, You know the truth!" - Baxter smirks at Cassandra.
"How Can you do this Baxter? How Can you………" - Cassandra replied.
"Can you see how famous I am right now! All the luxury you've been enjoying is because of this, So don't raise a finger on me."- Baxter yelled at Cassandra.

"Let me explain it to you darling! I made a pact with Satan Five years ago in exchange for fame and success. Now you became an obstacle to fulfilling my promise and that I could not let you come in between me and my pact. You have to accept my decision, as you have no other choice but I have to keep my promise to Satan." - Baxter replied

"Let us go! Let us go! Baxter, he is our child. How can you do this? Listen we can sort this out and will find a way but we can't do this to our child. Please listen to me, we don't need this luxury over our kid." - Cassandra begged him.

 Baxter stood over her, his eyes filled with anger and hatred. He raised his foot to kick her, Cassandra cried in pain but she was still begging him to save Rex, He again raised his foot to kick her but stopped when he heard a low growl behind him.
Turning around, he saw his son standing there, tears streaming down his face. "Dad, please stop," the boy pleaded. "Don't hurt Mom anymore."

Looking down at his wife, still writhing in pain on the floor, Baxter Replied - " Tell your Mom to be a good girl and do as Daddy said."
Kneeling down beside her, Rex gently helped her up, Through tear-filled eyes. Cassandra Could not even move, she felt like her ribs were broken and she was feeling immense pain in her chest.
She Slowly whispered near Rex - " Run Rex! Go and hide yourself down the street mommy will join you soon but promise me you will wait for mum to come. Go now and don't look behind, just run and hide yourself."

"Are we playing a game?" - Rex replied.
"Yes! "My baby and we have to win this game and we have to win against Daddy. Now do as I said." - Cassandra replied as tears welled up in her eyes as she realized the gravity of the situation.
Rex ran towards the front door and Baxter tried him to stop, while he was dragging him to lock him in his room, Cassandra put her all strength and tried to get up but her ribs cracked under the force of his fists. She tried hard and struggled to get a knife which was kept on the kitchen top and with tears streaming down her face, she lunged at Baxter, stabbing him in a desperate attempt to protect her Son. Baxter staggered back in shock, clutching at the wound in his leg. Rex, who had been cowering in fear, saw his chance to escape.

As he ran towards the door Baxter saw him and out of rage he slapped Cassandra and she fell next to the stove and unknowingly one of the gas knobs got activated. Cassandra fell on the floor and Baxter kicked her again against her chest, he unleashed his fury on her, beating her mercilessly until she passed out.

 He sighed constantly, feeling a sense of fulfillment and evilness wash over him. With a final gentle stroke of her hair, Baxtor leaned in and whispered, "I love you, Casssandra. You are my everything but it's time to say goodbye to you because no one can come in between my success, not even you."

He reached into his pocket and pulled out a pack of cigarettes, flicking one out and lighting it with a dramatic flourish., feeling the need to relieve some of the tension building up inside him. As he lit the cigarette, he took a deep drag and let out a sigh of relief. But little did he know that his actions would be his downfall. Unbeknownst to Baxtor, the gas stove in his kitchen had been leaking, slowly filling the room with a deadly gas. The lit cigarette in his hand unknowingly sparked a flame that quickly ignited the gas, causing a sudden explosion that engulfed the entire house in flames. His eyes widened in horror as he realized the danger he was in. But before he could react, the fire had already consumed him and Cassandra, burning them alive in a matter of seconds.

The neighbors heard the explosion and called the fire department, but by the time they arrived, it was too late. Rex, who was waiting for his mother, saw smoke billowing from his house. Panicked, Rex ran towards his home, only to find it engulfed in flames. His heart sank as he realized his mother and father were still inside. Tears streamed down his face as he stood helplessly outside, watching his home burn.

"Mom! Mom!" he cried out, hoping against hope that she would hear him and come running out. But there was no sign of her. The flames roared louder, consuming everything in their path. Neighbors gathered around, trying to comfort him as he sobbed uncontrollably.

Rex was taken by a police officer and brought to a nearby child care facility. He was in shock, his mind unable to comprehend what had just happened. He clung to the officer, begging to go back and find his mother and father. But it was too late. The fire had taken them away, leaving him alone and scared. The staff at the child care center tried their best to comfort him, but nothing could ease the pain of losing his parents in such a tragic way.

As I woke up from the dream, tears streamed down my cheeks. The images of destruction and chaos I had witnessed were still fresh in my mind. I knew what I had to do. I had to fight evil.

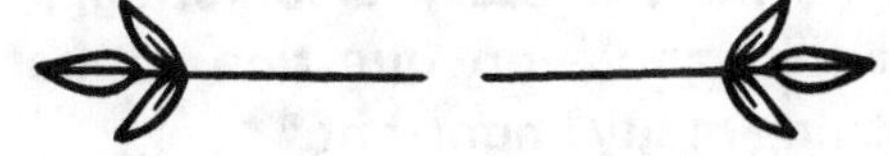

12

Now I know the truth about Rex's past and I knew his mother's soul gave me these glimpses to save her child from the evil spirit of Baxtor. Her spirit was not that strong enough to fight against his evil spirit and she wanted me to save his child's life. Am I capable enough to fight against the evil spirit of Baxtor? The devilish soul of Baxtor, now free from the confines of his human form, lurking behind Rex.

Mr.. Louis was standing next to me and asked me if I am fine to which I replied - " I want to tell you something, Please listen to me. I will answer each and every question but before that I want to tell you something really important."
"Please go on!" - Mr.. louis replied
"Mr.. Louis Rex is in danger and we have to save him." - I Replied
"Save him from whom? What are you talking about?" - Mr.. Louis replied
" When is Rex's birthday? We have to figure it out, where the file is in a hurry. We don't have time for Mr. Louis, we have to save him." - I replied in panic

Mr.. Louis held my hand and calmed me down and asked me "What is wrong with you? Can you please tell me what is going on?"
"Mr. Louis, you have to believe in what I am going to tell you now. I am a psychic medium, I have been gifted with the third eye where I can see and feel the spirits and channel their messages and the moment I touched the ledger the soul of Rex's mother pleaded with me to help her in saving his son's life." - I replied and told him everything I saw.
"You are overthinking Peace, I think you need some rest, you've been over exhausted, this is so unreal. Please go and take some

rest. We will talk later." - he replied
"I know you are not going to believe me but I don't have time for this. I have to save Rex. I want to know his birth date. Please help me Mr.. Louis we have to do something." - I replied

Mr... Louis turned around and searched his shelf which was behind his desk and pulled out a file which belonged to Rex.
"Here it is." - he replied and unfolded the file cover.
"His birthday is next month. He is turning Six! Oh boy! You were right , if I'm not wrong on his 6th birthday Mr.. Baxtor has pledged to sacrifice his soul to Satan. You were right, now what? We have only 16 days left how we gonna save him? " - he replied

It was the first time I had ever been at a loss for words. I stood there, staring blankly at the situation in front of me, unable to comprehend what had just happened. My mind was racing, trying to come up with a solution, but I was drawing a blank.

I tried to speak, to express my thoughts and feelings, but no words would come out. I felt completely overwhelmed, like I was drowning in a sea of confusion and uncertainty. How could I possibly cope with this situation when I couldn't even find the right words to express how I was feeling? But I knew I had to find a solution. I couldn't just stand there, helpless and mute. So I took a deep breath and closed my eyes, forcing myself to focus.

Determined to protect Rex from this malevolent force, I delved deeper into my psychic abilities. I knew I had to act swiftly to save him from the clutches of darkness.

My mind was focused and my heart filled with courage,
I embarked on a perilous journey to confront Baxtor's devil soul. Suddenly I felt a strange energy emanating from one particular name –Miss Hannah. She was the one who helped me in my childhood. I told Mr.. Louis that I have to leave for now and will call him later once I get a solution.

I came to my room and I opened my desk where I kept a wooden box which I had been wearing since i was a kid. The moment I took that in my hand it glowed, it never did like this before. I was again drawn to this name "Hannah" and felt a strong urge to know more about it. I called my mom. I asked her if she knew who Miss Hannah was.

To which she replied- " Oh! Dear I guess you have to know the truth , it's the right time for you. You remember I always made sure that you would wear that pendant to suppress your power. That was given to you by Miss Hannah when you were little. She told me that one day you will have come again searching for her when your powers were about to be fully evoked. You have to go to our old lake house. I am sending you Miss Hannah's address to find her and she will answer your every question. Please be safe, Peace." I could hear the worry and sadness in her voice. She hung up the phone and dropped me a text where she mentioned the address of Miss Hannah. I called Mr.. Louis and asked him to meet, to which he agreed and we met in the coffee shop nearby.

"Mr.. Louis, I have to leave for the old town tomorrow morning. From there I can get help." - I told Mr.. Louis to which he replied - " I am coming with you. There is no way that I will let you go alone."
"We don't have time Mr.. Louis, one has to be there with Rex to protect him. Please understand." - I replied.
"Rex is not alone here, a whole team is looking after him can't you see but i will not allow you to go alone. It is final that I am coming with you, you don't have any choice. We will be leaving tomorrow in the morning, packing your stuff and I will be waiting for you." - Mr.. Louis replied in a commanding way to which I agreed.

Next morning we left the Child Care home and started our journey to the Old Town. It took us a six hour drive and we were in the old town and you reached the address which mom gave us. As we arrived at the house, Entering the house, I was enveloped by a sense of nostalgia and familiarity. Memories flooded back. There was an eerie sense of something waiting to be discovered. As we wandered through the overgrown gardens, we stumbled upon a small, dilapidated cottage.

Inside the cottage there we saw old dusty crystals and faded tarot cards littered the table, and an ancient book sat on a pedestal covered in a red satin cloth. As I approached the book, I felt a surge of energy coursing through, filled with knowledge and power that I had never known before. With the ancient wisdom contained within its pages.

I found a note tucked on it. It was from Madame Hannah, As it was left for me to foresee my arrival. carefully unwrapped it, revealing a book filled with powerful spells to fight against the forces of evil. As I opened the note, It was written by herself, who had known that I would come for it one day. The note revealed that a talisman given to me in my childhood would serve as my protection against evil forces. She urged me to keep it close at all times.

The note ended with a powerful message: This is your journey, and you have been chosen to face challenges and help those in need. It is your destiny to aid the souls seeking peace and guide them on their path. "This is the Book of Shadows," she explained. "It contains powerful spells and ancient knowledge that can help you in your battles against the forces of darkness." "The book and the talisman are your tools, but it is your courage and compassion that will guide you."

With trembling hands, I untied the satin cloth and opened the book. As I turned the pages, I discovered intricate illustrations and handwritten instructions for various spells.

"I found it! Mr.. Louis this book will help us to save Rex. we have to leave now." - I told Mr.. Louis, who seemed stunned at that moment. I held his hand and brought him to the parked car. Mr.. Louis was still bewildered and he was not able to process anything. I motioned him to get into the car and we drove off to our destination. We didn't say anything to each other the whole way.

It took me a week and I read the whole book. With newfound determination and the book of spells in my possession, I embarked myself on an extraordinary adventure, ready to embrace the role as a protector. We were left with only three days and I started the rituals to protect Rex. Mr.. Louis informed Mrs. Martha and she also agreed to help us and we made a setup.

I started the ritual where a circle with salt was made in Rex's room and inside the circle I told everyone to be in, candles were placed around the circle and Mr.. Louis, Mrs. Martha, Rex along with me, we sat inside the circle. As I started enchanting the spells I saw the devilish soul of Baxtor. His eyes glowed with a sinister intent, as he plotted to take the boy's life and regain his lost power. Determined to protect Rex from this malevolent force, I delved deeper into my psychic abilities. I knew I had to act swiftly to save him from the clutches of darkness.

With my mind focused and my heart filled with courage, I embarked on a perilous journey to confront Baxtor's devil soul. I sought all my knowledge and powerful spells to banish the darkness that threatened Rex's life. I could sense the swirling darkness surrounding us, but I refused to let fear consume me. I channeled my energy, creating a protective shield around us.

In a climactic battle between good and evil, I unleashed my psychic abilities, casting spells and summoning ancient forces to banish Baxtor's devil soul. The room crackled with energy as the two forces clashed, each vying for control. Despite being banished, Baxtor's devil soul is far from finished. Consumed by vengeance, he sets his sights on me, determined to seek revenge.

Shadows dance menacingly around, whispers of his presence echoing in our ears. Now I find myself in a battle against an enemy which I thought I had vanquished. My psychic abilities are put to the test as I sense the malevolent energy surrounding us. I know I will face Baxtor once again, but this time, the stakes are higher than ever.

I perform the ritual with unwavering focus, calling upon the forces of light to aid us. As the ritual reaches its climax, a blinding light engulfs around us, dispelling the darkness that had plagued Rex. Baxtor's vengeful spirit is shattered and defeated, unable to harm Rex any longer. After an intense battle, we emerged victorious against the evil soul of Baxtor. Rex's mother appears before us. Grateful and at peace, she expresses her gratitude to me for bringing her closure and guiding her to the light and saving his kid.

Now, with a clear sense of purpose and feeling the need for self-discovery I decided to embark on a journey to further understand myself and my abilities. I found myself in a terrifying battle against an evil spirit that was once involved in satanic rituals. The stakes were high as the deal between this person and Satan was broken because of my intervention.

But as the saying goes, "Hell hath no fury like a demon scorned." Seeking revenge, I never knew that Satan would unleash an extreme evil entity upon me. I could feel its malevolent presence lurking in every corner. The dark aura started suffocating me. Little i know the battle was far from easy.

I found myself caught in the middle of a sinister deal between Satan, the embodiment of evil, and a guy named Baxtor. Satan, furious that Peace had disrupted his plans, decided to challenge me to a high-stakes showdown.

After battling with the evil spirit of Baxtor, I find myself completely drained of energy. In this crucial moment, I realized that I needed to prioritize my well-being and recharge my energy. I decided to take a career break and move back to my parents' house. It's a wise choice because being in a familiar and nurturing environment can help me regain my strength and find inner peace

At my parents' house, I surround myself with love and support. I spent time reconnecting with my family, sharing stories, and enjoying their company. They provide me with the comfort and encouragement I need to heal and replenish my energy. As time went by, I started to feel my energy returning. I gained a fresh perspective on life and my purpose.

While I was on my career break at my parents' house, I started feeling a chilling presence of an evil entity. It turns out that this entity is actually a satanic being, and it's rooting for me because I interfered in a deal between the satanic entity and Baxtor.

13

As I fumbled with the keys to my parents' house, struggling to find the right one in the dim light of the porch. As I finally clicked open the lock and stepped inside, a shiver ran down my spine. The air felt heavy and oppressive, as if something sinister lingered in the shadows.

Ignoring my unease, I made my way through the familiar rooms of the house, calling out for my parents. But there was no answer, only silence that seemed to echo through the empty halls. I felt a growing sense of dread as I realized I was completely alone.

Suddenly, a cold breeze swept through the room, causing the hairs on the back of her neck to stand on end. My heart pounded in my chest as I turned to see a dark figure standing in the corner, its eyes glowing with a malevolent light.

Fighting back a scream, I felt a surge of fear wash over me. But then, almost as if by instinct, I found myself raising my hand in front of me, a barrier of energy forming around me in a shimmering shield.

The entity snarled and lunged towards me, but it was met with an invisible force that pushed it back, causing it to howl in frustration. I stood to my ground, my eyes blazing with determination as I stared down the creature before me.

"You have no power here," I declared. My voice was steady and strong. "I am protected by forces you cannot comprehend. Leave this place, and do not return."

With a final roar of rage, the entity vanished into thin air, leaving me alone once more in the quiet house. I let out a shaky breath, my hand falling to my side as the shield dissipated around me.

As I gazed around the room, a sense of peace washed over. I knew I had faced something truly evil, but I had emerged victorious. And I knew that no matter what darkness may come my way, I would always have the strength to protect myself.

As I step into my room an eerie silence again fills the air. Suddenly, the temperature drops, and a chilling gust of wind rattles the windows. The presence of evil is so strong that it sends shivers down to my spine.

In the dimly lit room, shadows dance ominously, whispering secrets of darkness. Every creak of the floorboards echoes through the house, intensifying the sense of foreboding. My heart starts pounding in my chest as I realize that I am not alone.

Then, a flickering light catches my attention. As I follow it, I find myself in the basement, a place I never liked to venture into. The air grows heavy with an oppressive energy, and the sound of whispers grows louder. It's as if the very walls are conspiring against me.

Suddenly, a figure emerges from the darkness. It's the satanic entity, a menacing presence with glowing red eyes and a wicked grin. It taunts me, revealing its true intentions. It wants to use me as a pawn in its sinister game, to ensure the success of its deal with Baxtor.

Fear grips my heart, but I refuse to succumb to the darkness. With every ounce of courage, I confronted the entity, my voice trembling yet filled with determination. I call upon the power of love and light, channeling my inner strength to banish the evil that seeks to consume me.

The battle between good and evil rages on, each moment more intense than the last. Energy crackles in the air as I unleash my psychic abilities, pushing back against the satanic entity's malevolent influence. It's a fight for my very soul, a struggle that will test my resolve and resilience.

There before me stood a figure cloaked in black. His eyes glowed with an otherworldly light, and a wicked smile played on his lips. I could feel the malevolent energy emanating from him, and I knew in that moment that I was in the presence of a satanic entity.
"Why have you come here?" I tried to speak, but my words caught in my throat. I was paralyzed by fear and awe at the same time. Before I could muster a response, the entity let out a chilling laugh and vanished into thin air. I stood there, trembling, unsure of what just happened and what would happen next.

Days passed, and the memory of that encounter still haunts me. But then, in the dead of night, the entity reemerged, its presence filling the room with an overwhelming darkness. I could feel its icy gaze boring into my soul, and I knew that whatever was to come next would change me forever. The satanic entity had returned, and this time, I knew that there would be no escaping its grasp.

The room was filled with a thick, suffocating darkness as I watched in horror as Satan himself stood before me, his sinister grin sending chills down my spine. My mother lay helpless on the ground, her body wracked with pain as Satan's dark energy enveloped her.

I tried to muster every ounce of strength within me, but my powers were weak, depleted from the relentless battles I had fought against the forces of evil. I could only watch in agony as Satan raised his hand, a malicious light dancing in his eyes.

"No!" I screamed, my voice raw with desperation. "Please, don't do this! Take me instead!"

Tears streamed down her face as I pleaded with the devil himself, my voice filled with desperation and fear.

"Satan, please, I beg of you. Spare my mother's life. She didn't do anything. It was me, I swear," I whimpered, I clasped my hands together in a futile gesture of prayer.

But Satan's eyes burned with a fiery anger as he gazed down at me, a cruel smirk twisting his lips. "Mistake or not, your mother has sealed her fate. You have broken our deal, and now she must pay the price."

"No! Please, stop! Take me instead! Spare her life!"

But Satan only laughed, his cruel laughter echoing through the room like a dagger to my heart. He leaned down, his twisted face inches from my mother's, and with a swift motion, he plunged his dark hand into her chest.

I could hear my mother's agonized screams as Satan ripped her soul from her body, his evil devouring her light until she lay still, lifeless and empty. Tears streamed down my face as I fell to my knees, my heart shattered into a million pieces.

"I'm sorry, Mom," I whispered through sobs, my voice barely a whisper in the darkness. "I couldn't save you. I wasn't strong enough."

Satan turned his gaze toward me, his eyes burning with a malevolent fury. "Your time will come, child," he hissed, his voice like poison in my ears. "Your power may be weak now, but one day, I will come for you, and there will be no one to save you."

I trembled in fear as Satan disappeared into the shadows, leaving me alone with my mother's lifeless body. And in that moment, as the darkness closed in around me, I knew that my fight against evil had only just begun. And I swore that I would never again be powerless to save those I loved.

With my determination and bravery, I decided to confront the satanic entity head-on. I seek guidance from "The book of Shadows", against evil forces. I research ancient texts and consult with wise elders to find a way to protect myself from the satanic entity's malevolent influence and fight against him.

As I delve deeper into the mysteries of the supernatural, I uncover hidden powers within myself.

Tragically, the evil spirit took the life of my beloved mother, leaving me feeling helpless and filled with grief. But I, fueled by my determination and love for my mother, refused to sit idly by and let darkness prevail.

With a heavy heart, I embarked on a journey to confront the malevolent force that had taken so much from me. Armed with my unwavering courage and a newfound strength, I delved into the depths of the supernatural realm.

As I navigated through treacherous obstacles and encountered twisted creatures, I discovered hidden sources of power within myself. I learned ancient rituals and spells, harnessing the forces of light to combat the darkness that threatened to consume my identity.

But the battle was far from easy. The evil spirit taunted me, using my mother's memory as a weapon to weaken my resolve. Yet, I remained resolute, refusing to let despair cloud my judgment.

With each confrontation, I grew stronger, tapping into my inner strength and unleashing my righteous fury. I confronted the evil spirit head-on, using my newfound abilities to dismantle its malevolent influence.

The day came and I summoned the devil again in the old abandoned house that stood ominously in the darkness of the night, its windows broken and boarded up, its roof sagging and creaking in the wind. The air was thick with the stench of decay and decay, and a cold chill seemed to seep into the very bones of anyone who dared to approach.

As the wind howled and the trees rustled with an eerie whisper, a figure clad in dark robes emerged from the shadows. With a flick of their wrist, they lit a series of black candles that lined the steps leading up to the front door of the house.

Inside, the walls were covered in peeling wallpaper, and the floors creaked ominously underfoot. The only light came from the flickering flames of the candles, casting eerie shadows that danced around the room.

At the center of the room, a pentagram had been painted in dark red blood, and strange symbols adorned the walls. The figure in the dark robes moved to the center of the pentagram and began to chant in a guttural, otherworldly language.

Suddenly, the air grew thick with a sense of malevolence, and a dark presence seemed to descend upon the room. The figure in the robes continued to chant, the words growing louder and more urgent, until finally, with a deafening crack, a swirling vortex appeared in the center of the pentagram.

From the depths of the vortex, a creature emerged – its skin black as coal, its eyes glowing with a sinister light. It let out a chilling wail that echoed through the house.
The satanic entity had been summoned.

The room was dark, filled with an eerie sense of foreboding as I stood face to face with the satanic entity that had been terrorizing me for months. Its eyes glowed with a malevolent red light, and its twisted, demonic features sneered at me.

I could feel the weight of its presence pressing down on me, trying to crush my spirit and break my will. But I refused to back down. I knew that I had to stand my ground and fight back, no matter how powerful my adversary appeared to be.

I closed my eyes and reached deep within myself, tapping into the psychic abilities that I had always known were there, but had never fully embraced. I felt a surge of energy flow through me, empowering me and filling me with a sense of calm determination.

With a sudden burst of strength, I unleashed a psychic wave that sent the satanic entity reeling backwards. Its twisted form convulsed in agony as my psychic energy burned through its malevolent essence.

But the entity was not defeated so easily. It lashed out at me with dark tendrils of energy, trying to ensnare me and drag me down into the depths of darkness with it. I gritted my teeth and fought back with all of my psychic might, pushing back against the dark forces that threatened to overwhelm me.

As the battle raged on, I could feel myself getting weaker, my psychic reserves dwindling with each passing moment. But I refused to give up. I dug deep within myself, finding a hidden well of strength that I never knew I had.

With one final surge of psychic energy, I pushed back against the satanic entity with all of my might. I could feel it struggling against me, It's dark essence beginning to dissipate as my light overcame its darkness.

And then, with a final scream of agony, the entity vanished in a burst of blinding light. I stood alone in the room, breathing heavily and feeling the weight of my victory settle upon me.

I had faced the satanic entity and emerged victorious, using my psychic abilities to banish it from my life once and for all. I knew that there would always be dark forces out there, waiting to test me, but I also knew that I had the strength and the power to overcome them.

With a sense of pride and determination, I walked out of the room, ready to face whatever challenges awaited me in the future, knowing that I would never again be afraid to embrace my true psychic potential.

The rain poured down in heavy sheets, the sky crackling with lightning and thunder as I stood in the aftermath of my battle with the satanic entity that had been terrorizing the town for far too long. Blood soaked my clothes, both mine and the creature's, as I surveyed the destruction around me.

I dropped to my knees in the mud, tears mixing with the rain as the weight of what I had just done hit me. The screams of the innocent, the terror in their eyes as they ran from the demonic creature – it was all too much to bear. But I had done it. I had faced my fears head on and came out victorious.

But victory came at a cost. The scars, both physical and emotional, were etched deep into my soul. Would I ever be the same after this? Could I ever go back to the person I was before, unburdened by the knowledge of the darkness that lurked in the shadows?

As I struggled to catch my breath, a voice cut through the storm, soft and melodic. I looked up to see a figure standing in the distance, their face obscured by the rain. They reached out a hand to me, their eyes full of compassion and understanding.

"Come with me," the figure said, their voice gentle yet commanding. "There is much more work to be done, more evil to be vanquished. But you are not alone. Together, we can fight back against the darkness that threatens to consume us all."

I took the figure's hand, feeling a surge of power and determination coursing through me. I knew that my journey was far from over, that this was only the beginning. But I was ready. Ready to face whatever horrors awaited me, ready to stand against the forces of evil and protect those who could not protect themselves.

As I stood up, the rain washing away the blood and grime of battle, I knew that I had found my purpose. And though my heart ached for the lives lost and the innocence stolen, I knew that by fighting back against the darkness, I would be honoring their memories and ensuring that their sacrifices were not in vain.

With a final glance back at the scene of destruction, I followed the figure into the night, ready to take on whatever challenges lay ahead. The storm raged on, but I was no longer afraid. For I was a warrior now, and I would not rest until all souls were free from the clutches of evil.

I am ready for this new journey, ready to face the evil souls that haunt this world and help guide the lost souls to find peace. I know the danger that lies ahead, but I am determined to make a difference, to use my powers for good.

As I take a deep breath, the ground beneath me begins to shake. A dark energy swirls around me, causing my heart to race with fear. But I push the fear aside, drawing on the strength within me to face whatever lies ahead.

Suddenly, a group of evil souls appear before me, their eyes glowing with malevolent energy. They hiss and snarl, their twisted forms reaching out towards me. I raise my Talisman, ready to defend myself against their onslaught.

But before I can strike, a soft voice whispers in my ear. "Remember, not all souls are beyond redemption. Some are simply lost and in need of guidance." The words echo in my mind, reminding me of my true purpose.

I lower my Talisman, taking a step closer to the evil souls. "I offer you a chance at peace," I say, my voice steady and strong. "Let go of your anger and hatred, and embrace the light within you."

The evil souls falter, their eyes flickering with uncertainty. I extend a hand towards them, a small spark of light glowing at my fingertips. And to my surprise, they reach out and grasp it, their forms softening as the darkness begins to fade.

As the storm clouds part and the moon shines down upon us, I feel a sense of peace wash over me. I may have just begun this journey, but I know that I am on the right path. And as I continue on, I am determined to help as many souls as I can find their way back to the light.

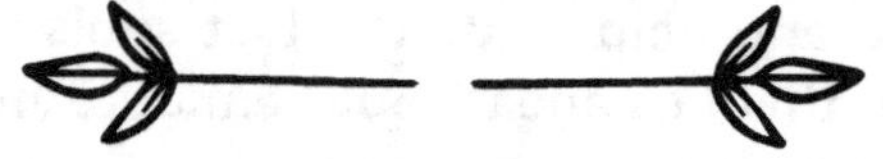